Cultured Urban Astrology

by Nina Strong

Contents

The Zodiac signs are associated with four elements, with each element representing different characteristics.

Here are the elements and the signs associated with them:

Fire Signs: Aries, Leo, Sagittarius Air Signs: Gemini, Libra, Aquarius Water Signs: Cancer, Scorpio, Pisces Earth Signs: Taurus, Virgo, Capricorn.

Fire signs are known for being passionate and energetic, air signs are for being intellectual and communicative, water signs are for being emotional and intuitive, and earth signs are for being practical and grounded.

As a little girl, I always found myself fascinated with the Planets, moons, and stars of our universe. I precisely started to study birthdays and characteristics of individuals as I matured into an adult and came to the conclusion that depending on your sun, rising, and moon differences based on the time you were born, most people had similar traits but not identical. In my book of astrology, you will get the chance to learn the 12 zodiac signs, male and female, and dive into the characteristics of each zodiac sign.

Aquarius: Ruled by Uranus, and an air sign, represents the Water Bearer.

Chapter 1

Aquarius: (January 20- February 18)

Male traits: Analytical, innovative, detached Influence of Uranus.

What's it like to date an Aquarius man? Dating an Aquarius man can be exciting and unique. They are known for their innovative thinking, independence, and intellect. They tend to like individuals who value freedom and individuality in relationships. Aquarius men appreciate stimulating conversations, debates, about ideas, and sharing intellectual pursuits. Show him that you are open-minded, creative, and willing to explore new ideas and experiences.

How to get an Aquarius man to fall in love with you?

Aquarius men value their independence and freedom, so it's important to give them space and respect their need for autonomy. Being supportive of his goals and aspirations, as well as encouraging his individuality, can help you win his heart. Additionally, Aquarius men are attracted to uniqueness and authenticity. Be yourself, express your true personality, and show him your quirks and interests. Embrace your own individuality and stand out from the crowd to capture the attention of an Aquarius man. Overall, building a strong intellectual connection, respecting his independence, and being authentic and unique are key ways to get an Aquarius man to fall in love with you.

Female traits: Independent, eccentric, humanitarian Influence of Uranus.

What's it like to date an Aquarius woman? Dating an Aquarius woman can be exciting and stimulating. Aquarius women are typically friendly, social, and open-minded individuals known for their unconventional and progressive nature. They often have a strong sense of justice and equality, and they may be passionate about humanitarian causes and social issues. Build a strong friendship, show her that you can be her confidante, ally, and supportive friend. Build an emotional connection by being understanding, caring, and committed to her well- being. By engaging her intellectually, respecting her independence, sharing common values, being authentic and unique, embracing adventure and spontaneity, and building a strong friendship, you can have her wrapped around your fingers.

How to get an Aquarius woman to fall in love with you?

It is crucial to understand and appreciate her unique qualities and values. Show that you respect her need for autonomy and individuality. Avoid being possessive and controlling. Allow her space to pursue her interests and passions. Embrace adventure and spontaneity. Aquarius women are adventurous and open to new experiences. They love to try new things in a relationship, so keep things fresh, exciting, and full of surprises. Overall, building a strong intellectual connection, respecting her space, and being authentic and creative are the key ways to get an Aquarius woman to fall in love with you.

Aquarius- The Water Bearer

The Water Bearer symbolizes innovation, humanitarian, and forward-thinking spirit. Aquarius individuals are often seen as visionaries who prioritize collective- well-being. They value originality and often thinking outside the box. The Water Bearer itself does not literally represent water but rather the act of pouring out knowledge, ideas, and insights to nurture and benefit society. The Water Bearer's association with water also symbolizes emotional depth and a connection to the universal flow of life.

The parts of the body associated with the Water Bearer are the calves, ankles, and the circulatory system. Foods

such as garlic, onion, fatty fish, beets, leafy greens and citrus fruits are a good source for the Aquarius.

Compatibility Analysis

1. Aquarius Man & Aries Woman

Compatibility: High

Dynamics: Both are energetic, innovative, and passionate. They share a love for independence and adventure. Their relationship is often lively and stimulating, with mutual respect for each other's individuality.

Challenges: Aries can be impulsive, which might clash with Aquarius's desire for freedom. Communication is key to maintain harmony.

2. Aquarius Man & Taurus Woman

Compatibility: Moderate

Dynamics: Taurus offers stability and practicality, which can ground Aquarius's unconventional nature. They can balance each other well if they appreciate their differences.

Challenges: Taurus's need for routine may conflict with Aquarius's love for novelty. Patience and understanding are needed.

3. Aquarius Man & Gemini Woman

Compatibility: Very High

Dynamics: Both are air signs, fostering excellent intellectual connection, communication, and shared curiosity. They enjoy socializing and exploring new ideas together.

Challenges: Both need to ensure emotional depth doesn't get overshadowed by their mental rapport.

4. Aquarius Man & Cancer Woman

Compatibility: Moderate

Dynamics: Cancer's nurturing qualities can contrast with Aquarius's detachment. However, their differences can complement each other if nurtured with understanding.

Challenges: Emotional compatibility can be tricky; Cancer seeks closeness, while Aquarius values independence.

5. Aquarius Man & Leo Woman

Compatibility: High

Dynamics: Both are confident, outgoing, and love attention. They can have a dynamic, exciting relationship filled with shared social activities.

Challenges: Both signs desire dominance; establishing mutual respect is essential.

6. Aquarius Man & Virgo Woman

Compatibility: Moderate

Dynamics: Virgo's practicality can help balance Aquarius's unconventional ideas. They can learn from each other.

Challenges: Virgo's critical nature might frustrate Aquarius's non-conformity.

7. Aquarius Man & Libra Woman

Compatibility: Very High

Dynamics: Both are air signs and value harmony, intellectual connection, and socializing. They enjoy mutual interests and are balanced partners.

Challenges: They should ensure their relationship remains dynamic and emotionally fulfilling.

8. Aquarius Man & Scorpio Woman

Compatibility: Challenging

Dynamics: Scorpio's intensity contrasts with Aquarius's aloofness. If they connect deeply, it can be transformative.

Challenges: Trust and emotional transparency are significant hurdles.

9. Aquarius Man & Sagittarius Woman

Compatibility: Excellent

Dynamics: Both love adventure, freedom, and exploration. They share a zest for life and can have a lively, fun-loving relationship.

Challenges: Both need to ensure consistency in their commitments.

10. Aquarius Man & Capricorn Woman

Compatibility: Moderate

Dynamics: Capricorn's discipline complements Aquarius's innovation. They can build a stable future together.

Challenges: Differences in approach to life and change require adjustment.

11. Aquarius Man & Aquarius Woman

Compatibility: Very High

Dynamics: Both are unconventional, independent, and forward-thinking. This pairing fosters a friendship-based romantic connection with mutual understanding.

Challenges: Both need to ensure their relationship doesn't become too detached or lack emotional depth.

12. Aquarius Man & Pisces Woman

Compatibility: Moderate to High

Dynamics: Pisces's compassion and imagination can inspire Aquarius, while Aquarius's originality can help Pisces express themselves.

Challenges: Emotional needs might differ; communication is vital.

Aries: An Aquarius woman and an Aries man share a vibrant, energetic connection rooted in mutual enthusiasm and independence. Both value freedom and are adventurous, which can lead to a stimulating relationship. The Aries man's boldness complements the Aquarius woman's innovative spirit, fostering excitement. However, their strong-willed natures may result in occasional clashes, but their shared zest for life usually keeps the relationship dynamic and engaging.

Taurus: This pairing can be challenging due to differing priorities. Taurus craves stability and comfort, while Aquarius seeks novelty and change. The Aquarius woman's unconventional approach may conflict with the Taurus man's need for security. However, if they appreciate each other's differences, they can learn from each other: she may introduce spontaneity, and he can help her ground her ideas. Patience and open-mindedness are key to forging a harmonious bond.

Gemini: An Aquarius woman and Gemini man often form a lively and intellectually stimulating partnership. Both are social, curious, and love engaging conversations, which keeps their connection fresh. Their shared love for novelty and ideas can lead to a supportive, fun relationship. Sometimes, their scattered energy might cause misunderstandings, but their mutual understanding and zest for learning help maintain harmony.

Cancer: This relationship can be a mix of warmth and detachment. Cancer seeks emotional security and nurturing, while Aquarius values independence and intellectual pursuits. The Aquarius woman might struggle to provide the emotional depth Cancer desires, and Cancer's sensitivity could feel overlooked. To succeed, both need to find common ground—Cancer can learn to give space, and Aquarius can develop emotional sensitivity.

Leo: When an Aquarius woman and Leo man come together, their relationship sparkles with creativity and mutual admiration. Both thrive on attention and excitement, making their partnership lively and optimistic. The Leo man's desire for romance and recognition complements the Aquarius woman's innovative spirit. However, pride or stubbornness could cause occasional clashes, but their shared energy typically ensures a passionate and fun connection.

Virgo: Compatibility between an Aquarius woman and Virgo man hinges on balancing practicality and idealism. Virgo's meticulous nature and desire for order may clash with the Aquarius woman's free-spirited and unconventional approach. Nevertheless, they can complement each other when they focus on mutual growth—she inspires new ideas, and he brings structure. Patience and understanding are vital for a harmonious bond.

Libra: This duo often cultivates a harmonious and balanced relationship. Both value fairness, social interactions, and intellectual stimulation. The Aquarius woman's innovative ideas blend well with Libra's diplomatic nature, leading to shared adventures and growth. Their mutual love for harmony enables them to navigate differences smoothly, creating a partnership grounded in mutual respect and companionship.

Scorpio: An Aquarius woman and Scorpio man experience a relationship with strong emotional undercurrents. Scorpio's depth and intensity can both intrigue and challenge the Aquarius woman, who prefers intellectual connections over emotional extremes. Trust and openness are essential. If they can navigate their differences, their relationship can evolve into a transformative experience marked by depth and mutual enlightenment.

Sagittarius: This pairing is often energetic and optimistic. Both love adventure, freedom, and new experiences, making their connection lively and spontaneous. The Sagittarius man's love for exploration complements the Aquarius woman's inventive nature. They motivate each other to grow and explore, making their relationship fun and inspiring. Occasional disagreements about commitment might arise but are generally resolved through shared enthusiasm.

Capricorn: An Aquarius woman and Capricorn man may initially seem contrasting—one values innovation and ideals, the other stability and tradition. However, their differences can be complementary; she inspires him with new ideas, and he offers structure. With patience and mutual respect, they can build a relationship that balances progress and stability, fostering growth and long-term partnership.

Aquarius: When two Aquarians come together, the relationship often thrives on shared ideals, intellectual stimulation, and independence. Both value freedom and innovation, which allows for a social, engaging union. Their mutual understanding of each other's need for space and self-expression fosters a relationship based on friendship and mutual growth, making it exciting and harmonious.

Pisces: An Aquarius woman and Pisces man can create a deeply compassionate and imaginative connection. Pisces' emotional sensitivity complements Aquarius' innovative outlook, leading to a romantic and idealistic bond. Challenges may arise from their different approaches to emotional expression—Pisces seeks closeness, while Aquarius values independence. Cultivating understanding allows their relationship to be both inspiring and nurturing.

Pisces: Ruled by Neptune and a water sign represents the Fishes.

Chapter 2

Pisces: (February 19 – March 20)

Male traits: Intuition, altruistic, creativity Influence of Neptune.

What's it like to date a Pisces man? Dating a Pisces man can be a dreamy and romantic experience. Pisces men are known for being compassionate, intuitive, and imaginative. They are sensitive souls who value emotional connections and deep conversations. It is important to appeal to his emotions and show him your own compassionate and understanding nature. Be genuine, empathetic, and supportive, as Pisces men appreciate authenticity and kindness. Embrace his creative side, as they tend to be artistic and enjoy finding beauty in the world around them. In a relationship with a Pisces man, you may find yourself swept off your feet by his romantic gestures and his ability to tune into your feelings. He may be empathetic and understanding, offering you emotional support and a listening ear whenever you need it.

How to get a Pisces man to fall in love with you?

Pisces men are highly empathetic and caring, so show that you understand and care about his feelings and emotions. Be your true self and avoid playing games or being insincere. They crave deep emotional connections, share your thoughts, dreams, and fears with him, and be willing to engage in a meaningful conversation. Pisces men are typically creative and artistic, by showing interest in his creative pursuits and encourage him to express himself through his art, he will start showing his expressions of love more. Respect his humility, and be genuine, By being supportive to these traits, you can capture the heart of a Pisces man.

Female traits: Empathetic, intuitive, spiritual Influence of Neptune.

What's it like to date a Pisces woman? Dating a Pisces woman can be a magical and fulfilling experience. They are often romantic dreamers who value emotional connections and spiritual depth in relationships. Pisces women can be sensitive and may need reassurance at times. Be patient, supportive, and understanding of her emotions, and be open and honest with your feelings and emotions.

How to get a Pisces woman to fall in love with you?

Be genuine, Pisces women love honesty, show your true self. They often are romantic dreamers who appreciate gestures of love and affection. Plan thoughtful dates, surprise her with small gifts, and express your feelings openly. Pisces women are often creative, so show interest in her artistic traits, whether it's music, art, or literature. By being genuine, empathetic, and supportive, you can get the heart of a Pisces woman and build a strong, lasting relationship based on mutual love and understanding.

Pisces- The Fishes

The Pisces are represented by two fishes swimming in opposite directions, symbolizing duality, intuition, and the complexity of emotions. Spiritual dueled nature Pisces are associated as a water sign are, a reflection of deep emotions and feelings. The Fishes are fluid creatures that can navigate a variety of environments, which reflects their adaptability and flexibility. Overall, the fish symbolizes the essence of the Pisces personality sensitive, compassionate, and deeply connected to the emotional and spiritual realms.

The body parts that are associated with The Fishes are the feet, and the lymphatic system. Foods such as dark leafy greens, cranberries, red cabbage, beets, cherries, and lean protein are good sources of Pisces.

Compatibility Analysis

1. Pisces Man & Aries Woman

Compatibility Overview: Moderate to Challenging

Details: Aries is energetic, assertive, and adventurous, while Pisces is gentle, dreamy, and sensitive. Aries may find Pisces too soft or escapist, while Pisces might feel overwhelmed by Aries' directness. However, their mutual passion can create a dynamic connection if both respect each other's differences.

Potential: Growth through patience and understanding—Pisces can help Aries soften, and Aries can motivate Pisces.

2. Pisces Man & Taurus Woman

Compatibility Overview: Very Good

Details: Both signs value stability, loyalty, and emotional depth. Taurus provides grounding, while Pisces offers emotional depth and compassion. Their shared love for homey comforts and art can foster a harmonious relationship.

Potential: Long-lasting bond, with mutual understanding and shared values.

3. Pisces Man & Gemini Woman

Compatibility Overview: Moderate

Details: Gemini is curious, lively, and communicative, while Pisces is intuitive and sensitive. Gemini may find Pisces too dreamy or elusive, and Pisces might find Gemini too restless or superficial. Successful communication is key to making this work.

Potential: They can learn from each other if open-minded.

4. Pisces Man & Cancer Woman

Compatibility Overview: Excellent

Details: Both are water signs, deeply emotional, intuitive, and nurturing. They understand each other's needs intuitively, creating a soulful, empathetic bond. This pairing tends to be very romantic and supportive.

Potential: Deep emotional connection and lasting partnership.

5. Pisces Man & Leo Woman

Compatibility Overview: Moderate to Challenging

Details: Leo is confident, expressive, and seeking admiration, while Pisces is soft, romantic, and often more reserved. Leo's desire for attention might clash with Pisces' sensitivity. However, Leo can inspire Pisces to be more assertive, and Pisces can soften Leo's ego.

Potential: Requires compromise and understanding.

6. Pisces Man & Virgo Woman

Compatibility Overview: Good

Details: Virgo's practicality complements Pisces' emotional sensitivity. They can create a balanced partnership—Virgo offering structure, Pisces providing emotional richness. Both are caring and service-oriented, which can foster harmony.

Potential: Stable, nurturing, and mutually supportive.

7. Pisces Man & Libra Woman

Compatibility Overview: Good to Very Good

Details: Libra seeks harmony and partnership, while Pisces craves deep emotional connection. Their shared love for beauty and art can enhance their bond. Occasionally, Libra's indecisiveness can frustrate the sensitive Pisces.

Potential: Romantic and balanced relationship if committed.

8. Pisces Man & Scorpio Woman

Compatibility Overview: Excellent

Details: Both are water signs, intensely emotional, intuitive, and passionate. Scorpio's depth aligns perfectly with Pisces' sentimental nature. They often share profound understanding and empathy.

Potential: Emotionally transformative and powerfully intimate bond.

9. Pisces Man & Sagittarius Woman

Compatibility Overview: Moderate

Details: Sagittarius is adventurous, freedom-loving, and optimistic, which can contrast with Pisces' dreamy, gentle nature. Sagittarius might find Pisces too elusive; Pisces may feel overwhelmed by Sagittarius' need for independence.

Potential: Needs open communication and boundaries.

10. Pisces Man & Capricorn Woman

Compatibility Overview: Moderate

Details: Capricorn is pragmatic and disciplined, while Pisces is imaginative and emotional. They can balance each other's strengths if willing to understand different approaches. Capricorn provides stability; Pisces offers emotional depth.

Potential: Potential for growth through patience.

11. Pisces Man & Aquarius Woman

Compatibility Overview: Challenging

Details: Aquarius values independence and innovation, whereas Pisces is more dreamy and emotionally expressive. Their differing nature can lead to misunderstandings unless they find common ground.

Potential: Encourage mutual understanding and respect.

12. Pisces Man & Pisces Woman

Compatibility Overview: Excellent

Details: Shared emotional depth and intuitive understanding make this a very harmonious pairing. Both may be highly empathetic and nurturing, creating a soulful connection. Potential pitfalls include escapism; mutual support is essential.

Potential: Deeply intuitive, romantic, and fulfilling relationship.

Aries: A Pisces woman may find an energetic and adventurous Aries man exciting, but their differences can lead to misunderstandings. Aries's directness might overwhelm sensitive Pisces, but their shared passion can forge a dynamic connection if mutual respect is maintained. Patience from Pisces balances Aries's impulsiveness.

Taurus: Both signs value stability and loyalty, making this pairing quite harmonious. A Taurus man's practicality complements a Pisces woman's dreamy nature, creating a nurturing and dependable bond. They enjoy building a comfortable, secure life together, with Taurus providing grounding and Pisces adding emotional depth.

Gemini: The intellectual and playful qualities of Gemini can intrigue a Pisces woman, fostering lively conversations and shared curiosity. However, Gemini's need for variety might clash with Pisces' longing for emotional intimacy. With effort, they can learn from each other—Gemini bringing lightness and Pisces offering soulful connection.

Cancer: Cancer and Pisces are both Water signs, which often creates an emotionally intuitive and empathetic partnership. They deeply understand each other's feelings, fostering a nurturing environment. Their shared sensitivity and focus on emotional security can make this a profoundly caring and supportive relationship.

Leo: Leo's boldness and love for admiration can excite a Pisces woman, who appreciates genuine kindness and creativity. However, Leo's need for attention might sometimes overshadow Pisces' gentle nature. Balance comes from mutual admiration and respecting each other's unique expressions of love.

Virgo: A Virgo man's analytical and organized tendencies can complement the artistic and intuitive qualities of a Pisces woman. Their pairing can result in a balanced mix of practicality and imagination. Communication and understanding are key to overcoming differences in approach to life.

Libra: Libra's charm and pursuit of harmony align well with Pisces' gentle, romantic nature. They both value love and connection, often creating a peaceful and affectionate relationship. Their shared appreciation for beauty and harmony helps sustain mutual understanding and admiration.

Scorpio: This can be an intensely emotional and transformative pairing. Scorpio's passion and depth resonate with Pisces' sensitivity, fostering a profound bond. However, both need to manage their emotional intensity and possessiveness to avoid conflicts and deepen trust.

Sagittarius: Sagittarius' adventurous spirit and love for exploration can inspire a Pisces woman, encouraging her to step outside her comfort zone. Conversely, Pisces provides emotional grounding that balances Sagittarius' impulsiveness. Together, they can explore both the world and their feelings.

Capricorn: A Capricorn man's ambition and practicality might seem distant to a dreamy Pisces woman, but their differences can complement each other well. Capricorn provides stability while Pisces nurtures the emotional, creative aspects of life, creating a balanced partnership if they communicate effectively.

Aquarius: Aquarius' innovative ideas and independence can intrigue a Pisces woman, fostering a relationship built on mutual respect for each other's individuality. Their shared love for ideals and humanitarian values can create a meaningful bond, though they need to honor each other's emotional needs.

Pisces: When two Pisces come together, their deep emotional understanding and shared creativity can lead to a magical and intuitive connection. They often intuitively meet each other's needs, forming a highly spiritual and compassionate bond that thrives on empathy and shared dreams.

Aries: Ruled by Mars and a Fire sign thats represented by the Ram.

Chapter 3

Aries: (March 21- April 19)

Male Traits: assertive, adventurous, competitive Influence of Mars.

What is it like to date an Aries Man? Well, let's start off by saying they have a passionate spirit. They are known for their love of adventure and excitement. They thrive on new experiences, so be prepared for spontaneous outings and fun activities. One thing I always find attractive in a man is confidence, and that's one thing that an Aries man will exude. They also take the lead in the relationships naturally. When they are interested, Aries men can put a lot of energy into their romantic endeavors. Aries men tend to be straightforward and honest. They appreciate clarity and dislike mind games, so be open with communication with these men.

While they love companionship, they also need personal space, they don't want to feel restricted.

How to get an Aries man to fall in love with you?

My suggestion is to be confident. Show that you are self-assured and secure in who you are, this will attract him and keep his interest.Engage in activities that spark excitement like hiking, traveling, hunting. Sharing adventures can deepen your connection. Keep it fun with humor; An Aries man appreciates a partner who can keep things fun. Last but not least, encourage his ambitions. Show interest in his goals and support his ambitions.

Female Traits: Bold, independent, passionate Influence of Mars

What is it like to date an Aries woman? Dating an Aries women can be a thrilling and dynamic experience. Aries women are known for their high energy and zest for life. They bring excitement and enthusiasm into relationships, making every moment feel vibrant and alive. Aries women value their independence. They are assertive and often know what they are, both in love and life. Communication tends to be direct and open with Aries women. She values honesty and transparency in relationships, which helps avoid misunderstandings. Aries women have a playful side and enjoys flirting. She often engages in light teasing and enjoys a bit of competition in her relationships. When she loves, she loves fiercely. She can be very passionate and intense in her feelings, often bringing a lot of emotion into the relationship.

How to get an Aries woman to fall in love with you?

Show passion when expressing your feelings, and be sincere. Aries women love to feel deeply and appreciates partners who can match their intensity. Be supportive, encourage her dreams, and help her pursue her passions. Showing that you believe in her ambitions will deepen your connection and make her feel cherished. By understanding and appreciating her dynamic nature, you can create a meaningful connection with an Aries woman. If you can keep up with her energy and match her passion for life, she'll likely find you irresistible!

Aries- Ram

The Ram symbolizes leadership, courage, determination, and assertiveness. Aries individuals are often seen as adventurous and pioneering, embodying the forward-driving spirit of the Ram. The Ram's association with the head (in terms of physical traits) suggests a strong-willed nature and the ability to charge ahead with boldness and confidence. The Ram's physical characteristics- strong, bold, and sometimes headstrong symbolizing the assertive nature of Aries individuals. They are known for their straightforwardness and willingness to take risks, often charging ahead into new experiences.

The part of the body that Aries is associated with is the head and upper body, particularly the face and brain. Foods such as oily fish like salmon, berries, nuts, whole grains, and leafy green vegetables are a good source for the head strong Ram.

Compatibility Analysis

1. Aries Man & Aries Woman

Compatibility: High energy, enthusiasm, and passion. Both desire independence and excitement.

Strengths: Mutual understanding of drive and ambition.

Challenges: Potential for rivalry and impulsiveness, leading to conflicts if not managed well.

Tips: Focus on maintaining mutual respect and independence; balance passion with patience.

2. Aries Man & Taurus Woman

Compatibility: Mixed. Taurus' steadiness can ground Aries, but differences may cause clashes.

Strengths: Taurus provides stability, while Aries brings spontaneity.

Challenges: Aries' impulsiveness may upset Taurus' need for security.

Tips: Build patience and appreciate each other's strengths; communication is key.

3. Aries Man & Gemini Woman

Compatibility: Very good. Both are energetic, communicative, and love adventure.

Strengths: Shared curiosity fosters excitement and mental stimulation.

Challenges: Both can be restless, potentially leading to superficiality or inconsistency.

Tips: Keep variety in the relationship and nurture emotional depth alongside fun.

4. Aries Man & Cancer Woman

Compatibility: Moderately challenging. Cancer seeks emotional security; Aries seeks independence.

Strengths: Can learn from each other—Cancer offers emotional depth, Aries brings dynamism.

Challenges: Differences in emotional expression, potential for misunderstandings.

Tips: Patience and understanding are essential; balance independence with emotional connection.

5. Aries Man & Leo Woman

Compatibility: Excellent. Both are passionate, energetic, and love attention.

Strengths: Mutual admiration, shared love for adventure and romance.

Challenges: Pride may cause conflicts; both desire leadership.

Tips: Respect each other's ego and work together as a team.

6. Aries Man & Virgo Woman

Compatibility: Moderate. Virgo's practicality can contrast Aries' impulsiveness.

Strengths: Virgo offers stability and detail orientation, balancing Aries' spontaneity.

Challenges: Aries may find Virgo overly critical or reserved.

Tips: Communicate openly; appreciate each other's different qualities.

7. Aries Man & Libra Woman

Compatibility: Good. Libra's social grace complements Aries' boldness.

Strengths: Both love socializing, romance, and excitement.

Challenges: Libra's indecisiveness can frustrate Aries' impulsivity.

Tips: Find common ground in social activities and decision-making.

8. Aries Man & Scorpio Woman

Compatibility: Intense. Both are passionate and driven.

Strengths: Deep emotional connection can develop.

Challenges: Power struggles, jealousy, and control issues.

Tips: Foster trust and honesty; respect emotional boundaries.

9. Aries Man & Sagittarius Woman

Compatibility: Excellent. Both are adventurous, optimistic, and love exploring.

Strengths: Great match for shared adventures and independence.

Challenges: Can be commitment-phobic; need to cultivate emotional intimacy.

Tips: Balance freedom with connection; respect each other's independence.

10. Aries Man & Capricorn Woman

Compatibility: Moderate. Capricorn's discipline contrasts with Aries' spontaneity.

Strengths: Capricorn's ambition can match Aries' drive.

Challenges: Differences in approach to risk and planning.

Tips: Cultivate mutual respect for differing priorities.

11. Aries Man & Aquarius Woman

Compatibility: Very good. Both are innovative and love freedom.

Strengths: Stimulating intellectual connection and mutual independence.

Challenges: Both may prioritize independence over intimacy.

Tips: Communicate openly; cherish friendship and adventure.

12. Aries Man & Pisces Woman

Compatibility: Challenging. Pisces' sensitivity contrasts with Aries' directness.

Strengths: Can balance each other's emotional energies.

Challenges: Aries' assertiveness may overwhelm Pisces; emotional misunderstandings.

Tips: Foster empathy and gentle communication.

Aries: This pairing is marked by high energy, mutual enthusiasm, and a shared zest for adventure. Both are fiery and passionate, which can lead to a dynamic relationship full of excitement. However, their strong personalities might lead to clashes unless they learn to compromise.

Taurus: Though differently tempered—the Aries woman's impulsiveness versus the Taurus man's steadiness—this relationship can balance out if they respect each other's pace. The Taurus man offers stability, while the Aries woman brings passion, making for a foundation that can either flourish or face challenges from stubbornness.

Gemini: A lively and intellectually stimulating pair, both signs love adventure, variety, and stimulation. Their relationship often thrives on fun and spontaneous activities, but it requires effort to maintain emotional depth and avoid superficiality.

Cancer: The attentive and nurturing Cancer may find the fiery Aries woman challenging, as her independence contrasts with Cancer's need for emotional security. Success depends on mutual understanding; if they bridge their differences, they can learn from each other's strengths.

Leo: Both are fiery and love to be the center of attention, which can ignite a passionate and vibrant romance. Their shared enthusiasm and confidence foster mutual admiration, creating a highly energetic and affectionate bond.

Virgo: An interesting mix of fire and earth, their compatibility relies on patience and understanding. While the Aries woman's impulsiveness may clash with the Virgo man's analytical nature, they can complement each other if they appreciate their differences.

Libra: Opposites attract here, with Libra's diplomacy balancing Aries' boldness. The relationship is often charming and romantic, but it may face challenges in decision-making, as Libra seeks harmony and Aries desires action.

Scorpio: Both are intense and passionate, leading to a powerful and transformative connection. However, their strong wills can cause conflicts unless they find ways to channel their energy constructively and build trust.

Sagittarius: A natural match for adventure lovers, both share a love for exploration, spontaneity, and independence. Their relationship tends to be fun-filled and optimistic, with mutual encouragement for personal growth.

Capricorn: This pairing combines fire and earth, which can either complement or clash. The Capricorn's discipline steadies the Aries woman's impulsiveness, and if they respect each other's drive, they can build a lasting partnership.

Aquarius: Innovative and energetic, this couple often enjoys unconventional pursuits together. Their shared love for novelty and independence makes for a stimulating relationship, but they need to stay grounded emotionally.

Pisces: The gentle and compassionate Pisces can soften the fiery Aries woman, creating a nurturing partnership. Although their differences are significant, mutual empathy and understanding can foster deep emotional connection.

Taurus: Ruled by Venus and an Earth sign thats represented by the Bull.

Chapter 4

Taurus: (April 20- May 20)

Male Traits: stable, reliable, sensual Influence of Venus.

What its like to date a Taurus man? Dating a Taurus man can be a rewarding experience marked by stability, sensuality, and loyalty. Taurus men are known for their dependable nature. They seek long-term stability and are often committed partners who value consistency in relationships. They appreciate the pleasures of life, including physical affection, good food, and comfort. A Taurus man tends to be romantic and enjoys creating intimate experiences with his partner. A Taurus man are patient but can also be very determined. Once they set their sights on something or someone, they pursue it with tenacity. They have a practical approach to life and relationships. Taurus men often prioritize tangible and realistic aspects, making thoughtful choices rather than impulsive ones. Most of us, not all, Taurus men have a taste for luxury and beauty. They appreciate quality and may have a keen interest in art, music, or gourmet food. While they are loyal, Taurus men can also be possessive in relationships. They value security and may be protective of their loved ones.

How to get a Taurus man to fall in love with you?

I say being authentic is a crucial part of getting a Taurus man to fall for you. You should be genuine in your interactions, and dont feel the need to put on a show. Taurus men appreciate honesty and straightforwardness. Create a comfortable environment of love and security. They love warm and inviting atmospheres, whether its in your home or during dates. Engaging in cozy activities can foster intimacy. Be affectionate to his needs, like small gestures of love, such as holding hands, cuddling, or giving thoughtful gifts, can strengthen your bond. Plan dates that appeal to his senses, such as cooking a delicious meal, enjoying a picnic in nature, or visiting galleries. You will do your best by engaging in activities that excite his appreciation for beauty and pleasure. Taurus men usually take their time when committing, so be patient as he evaluates the relationship, and don't rush him into making decisions. Show him that you're serious about the relationship by having conversations about future goals and aspirations. This could help him see your potential together. Taurus men value their personal space and independence, so allow him space without feeling pressured, this will show him you trust him. By understanding the Taurus man's nature and creating a supportive, affectionate environment, you can develop a strong and meaningful relationship. His loyalty and love can be deeply rewarding when nurtured with care and patience!

Female Traits: nurturing, practical, affectionate Influence of Venus.

Whats its like to date a Taurus woman? Dating a Taurus woman can be a rewarding enriching experience Taurus women are known for their loyalty. Once they commit to a relationship, they are usually dependable partners. Taurus women appreciate physical touch and often express their love through affection, they love romantic gestures and appreciates a partner who loves closeness. Many Taurus women enjoy the luxury things in life so they tend to love being surrounded by beauty and comfortable settings. If you appreciate her loyalty in-return, the relationship will lead to a strong, lasting relationship.

How to get a Taurus woman to fall in love with you?

Winning the heart of a Taurus woman can take some time and effort, but its definitely possible. Taurus women

often take their time in relationships. With a Taurus woman, you have to invest time and genuine interest. They value stability and security, so you'll probably want to show her your dependable and reliable. Trust is crucial for Taurus, so be honest and consistent to build a solid foundation. Authenticity is the goal for these women. Show her who you really are, be patient, and enjoy the journey.

Taurus- The Bull

The Bull represents strength, determination, and stability. The Bull symbolizes the steadfastness and grounded nature of Taurus individuals, who are often see as loyal and focused. Taurus the Ram is known for power, fertility, and abundance, and the love for comfort and luxury. The strong, sturdy nature of the Bull reflects Taurus's grounded personality and their connection to the earth. Additionally, the Bull signifies an appreciation for the finer things in life and a desire for stability and security in their relationship and surroundings.

The part of the body that the Taurus is associated with is the throat, neck, and ears. Foods rich in vitamins A, C, and E are essential, and foods like zinc-rich foods, leafy greens, citrus fruits, nuts, and berries are a good source for the Bull.

Compatibility Analysis

1. Taurus Man + Aries Woman

Compatibility: Moderate

Strengths: The Taurus man's calm and grounded nature can balance the Aries woman's fiery, impulsive energy. Both are determined and passionate, which can create a strong bond.

Challenges: Taurus's slow pace may frustrate Aries, who craves excitement and spontaneity. Aries's bluntness can also hurt Taurus's sensitive side.

Key to Success: Patience and compromise. Taurus needs to embrace Aries's adventurous spirit, while Aries should respect Taurus's need for stability.

2. Taurus Man + Taurus Woman

Compatibility: High

Strengths: Both value loyalty, stability, and comfort. They share similar goals and enjoy the finer things in life. Their connection is deeply sensual and harmonious.

Challenges: Stubbornness can lead to standoffs, and both may resist change.

Key to Success: Open communication and flexibility. They need to avoid power struggles and find ways to keep the relationship fresh.

3. Taurus Man + Gemini Woman

Compatibility: Low to Moderate

Strengths: Taurus's stability can ground Gemini's flighty nature, while Gemini's wit and charm can entertain Taurus.

Challenges: Taurus craves routine, while Gemini thrives on variety. Taurus may find Gemini inconsistent, and Gemini may see Taurus as too predictable.

Key to Success: Finding common interests and respecting each other's differences. Taurus should give Gemini space, while Gemini should appreciate Taurus's reliability.

4. Taurus Man + Cancer Woman

Compatibility: High

Strengths: Both are nurturing, loyal, and value emotional security. Taurus provides stability, while Cancer offers emotional depth and care.

Challenges: Taurus's stubbornness can clash with Cancer's moodiness.

Key to Success: Emotional honesty and mutual support. Both need to communicate openly and nurture their emotional bond.

5. Taurus Man + Leo Woman

Compatibility: Moderate to High

Strengths: Both enjoy luxury and romance. Taurus admires Leo's confidence, while Leo appreciates Taurus's loyalty and sensuality.

Challenges: Leo's need for attention may clash with Taurus's quiet nature. Both can be stubborn.

Key to Success: Mutual admiration and compromise. Taurus should show Leo affection, while Leo should respect Taurus's need for peace.

6. Taurus Man + Virgo Woman

Compatibility: High

Strengths: Both are practical, loyal, and detail-oriented. They share similar values and enjoy building a stable, harmonious life together.

Challenges: Virgo's perfectionism may irritate Taurus, who prefers to relax.

Key to Success: Appreciating each other's strengths and maintaining a balance between work and relaxation.

7. Taurus Man + Libra Woman

Compatibility: Moderate

Strengths: Both appreciate beauty, romance, and harmony. Taurus's stability can balance Libra's indecisiveness.

Challenges: Taurus's stubbornness may clash with Libra's desire for compromise. Libra's flirtatious nature may also make Taurus jealous.

Key to Success: Building trust and finding common ground. Taurus should be more flexible, while Libra should reassure Taurus of her loyalty.

8. Taurus Man + Scorpio Woman

Compatibility: High

Strengths: Both are passionate, loyal, and value deep emotional connections. Their relationship is intense and transformative.

Challenges: Scorpio's possessiveness may clash with Taurus's stubbornness. Both can be controlling.

Key to Success: Honesty and mutual respect. They need to trust each other and avoid power struggles.

9. Taurus Man + Sagittarius Woman

Compatibility: Low to Moderate

Strengths: Sagittarius's adventurous spirit can inspire Taurus, while Taurus's stability can ground Sagittarius.

Challenges: Taurus's love for routine may clash with Sagittarius's need for freedom. Sagittarius's bluntness may hurt Taurus's feelings.

Key to Success: Embracing each other's differences. Taurus should be open to adventure, while Sagittarius should appreciate Taurus's loyalty.

10. Taurus Man + Capricorn Woman

Compatibility: High

Strengths: Both are practical, ambitious, and value long-term commitment. They share similar goals and work well as a team.

Challenges: Both can be overly focused on work and may neglect romance.

Key to Success: Balancing work and play. They need to prioritize their emotional connection and enjoy life together.

11. Taurus Man + Aquarius Woman

Compatibility: Low

Strengths: Taurus's stability can ground Aquarius, while Aquarius's creativity can inspire Taurus.

Challenges: Taurus's traditional nature may clash with Aquarius's unconventional approach. Aquarius's detachment may frustrate Taurus.

Key to Success: Finding common interests and respecting each other's individuality. Taurus should be open-minded, while Aquarius should show more affection.

12. Taurus Man + Pisces Woman

Compatibility: High

Strengths: Both are romantic, sensitive, and value emotional connection. Taurus provides stability, while Pisces offers creativity and compassion.

Challenges: Pisces's dreaminess may clash with Taurus's practicality.

Key to Success: Supporting each other's needs. Taurus should embrace Pisces's imagination.

Aries: A Taurus woman and Aries man can experience a fiery attraction, but their differing temperaments may pose challenges. Taurus's steady, patient nature might clash with Aries's impulsiveness, but their mutual determination can help them overcome obstacles. If they learn to appreciate each other's strengths—Taurus's reliability and Aries's enthusiasm—they can create a passionate yet stable partnership.

Taurus: Two Taurus individuals together tend to enjoy a harmonious, comforting relationship based on shared values, loyalty, and love for the finer things in life. However, they must be mindful of potential stubbornness and complacency. Their mutual understanding can foster a deep, enduring bond built on trust and mutual appreciation.

Gemini: Taurus and Gemini have contrasting energies—Taurus's groundedness versus Gemini's adaptability. While Gemini's spontaneity can sometimes make Taurus feel uneasy, their differences can be complementary if they communicate well. Gemini brings spice and variety, while Taurus provides stability, making their relationship dynamic if both remain open-minded.

Cancer: A Taurus woman and Cancer man often form a nurturing, emotionally fulfilling pair. Both value home, security, and loyalty, creating a strong foundation. Their mutual understanding and caring nature foster deep emotional bonds, making this a typically harmonious pairing with devoted partnership prospects.

Leo: Taurus and Leo can share a love for luxury and admiration, but their personalities differ significantly. Taurus's practicality may clash with Leo's need for attention and dramatics. However, with mutual respect and understanding, Leo's warmth can soften Taurus's stubbornness, leading to a passionate and glamorous relationship.

Virgo: Virgo and Taurus are both earth signs, making their compatibility grounded and stable. They appreciate routine, cleanliness, and practical matters, often leading to a harmonious, hardworking partnership. Their shared values promote trust, though they must avoid becoming overly critical of each other.

Libra: Taurus and Libra can enjoy a charming, romantic relationship. While Taurus seeks stability and routine, Libra yearns for balance and social harmony. If they can navigate their different approaches—Taurus's practicality and Libra's idealism—they can build a graceful, aesthetically pleasing partnership.

Scorpio: This pairing can be intense and passionate. Taurus's steadfastness complements Scorpio's depth and emotional intensity. Both crave loyalty and security, creating a relationship with strong emotional bonds. Challenges may arise from Scorpio's possessiveness or Taurus's stubbornness, but mutual trust can sustain their connection.

Sagittarius: Taurus and Sagittarius have contrasting outlooks—grounded versus adventurous. While Taurus values stability and routine, Sagittarius seeks freedom and exploration. If they find common ground and respect each other's differences, they can enjoy a relationship that balances security with adventure, though patience may be required.

Capricorn: Both are ambitious earth signs, making Taurus and Capricorn highly compatible. They share a focus on goals, stability, and long-term planning. Their mutual ambition and work ethic can lead to a deeply committed, supportive partnership that thrives on shared values and mutual respect.

Aquarius: Taurus and Aquarius have distinct approaches—grounded versus unconventional. While Taurus prefers familiar routines, Aquarius seeks innovation and change. With effort, they can learn from each other; Taurus can introduce stability to Aquarius's ideas, and Aquarius can help Taurus embrace change and new perspectives.

Pisces: Taurus and Pisces often create a gentle, romantic duo. Taurus's practicality balances Pisces's dreaminess, resulting in a nurturing and imaginative relationship. Their mutual compassion and love for beauty foster a deep emotional connection, making this pairing tender and symbiotic.

Gemini: Ruled by Mercury and an Air sign that represents the Twins.

Chapter 5

Gemini: (May 21- June 20)

Male Traits: charming, inquisitive, communicative Influence of Mercury.

What's it like to date a Gemini Man? Dating a Gemini man can be an exciting and intellectually stimulating experience. Gemini men are known for their charm, wit, and adaptability. They are often very social and enjoy meeting new people. They thrive in social settings and often have a wide circle of friends. These men are known for curiosity and love to learn new things. They enjoy engaging in deep conversations and making intellectual stimulation in a relationship. Gemini men have a playful side, often using humor and wit to keep things light and entertaining, so they will appreciate a partner who can share the same sense of fun and spontaneity. They're also changeable in nature, they can be indecisive or change their mind frequently, which sometimes can lead to unpredictability in relationships. While Gemini men also enjoy companionship, they also value their independence and freedom. They need their space to pursue individual interests. Foster an open and honest communication, share your thoughts and feelings, and encourage him to do the same. Gemin men values a partner who articulates their emotions for him, so be direct.

How to get a Gemini man to fall in love with you?

Show that you're flexible and can go along with the flow. Plan fun, spontaneous outings, and be willing to try new things. This can keep the relationship exciting for him. Embrace the playful side of relationship! Use humor to create an enjoyable atmosphere. Gemini men love to laugh and appreciate a partner who can make them smile. Understand that his dual nature may lead to mood swings or inconsistencies, approach any changes in behavior with patience and an open mind, rather than frustration. By embracing the characteristics that define a Gemini man and creating an environment filled with intellectual stimulation and fun ,can establish a deep and meaningful connection that could lead to a lasting relationship!

Female Traits: witty, adaptable, social Influence of Mercury.

Whats it like to date a Gemini woman? Gemini women are typically vibrant social butterflies. They love to engage in meeting new people and exploring new places if they are feeling at their best. A Gemini woman tends to be very curious and loves learning new things.

She appreciates deep conversations and enjoys discussing various topics. Gemini women have a playful side and enjoy joking and teasing. They appreciate humor and love partners who can engage with them in lighthearted banter. She's likely just like a Gemini male to have a dual personality based on the twin trait, which means her moods can shift quickly. Because of her changeable nature, this could lead to unpredictability, and she might start to become indecisive and easily bored.

How to get a Gemini woman to fall in love with you?

Engage her in intellectually stimulating conversations. Share your interest about her, ask questions building a strong mental connection is crucial for her attraction. Keep the atmosphere light and enjoyable. Surprise her with spontaneous plans and outings. Attend social gatherings, meet her friends, and be an active participant in her social life. Understand that her moods and desires may fluctuate approach any changes with patience and an open mind, adapting to her whims as needed. By tapping into the characteristics that define a Gemini woman and creating an engaging, fun, and communicative relationship, you can develop a connection that she will cherish!

Gemini- The Twins

The Twins are associated with the idea of two sides, this can reflect conflicting traits, such as being social yet introverted. The Twins also represent versatility and adaptability. They can adjust to different situations and people effortlessly, often displaying a variety of interest and talent. Overall, the Twins encapsulate the essence of Gemini's vibrant and multifaced nature, represented the various traits that characterize this sign.

The parts of the body that Gemini is associated with are the lungs, shoulders, arms, and hands. Foods such as apples, beats, leafy greens, and lentils are a great source for the Twins.

Compatibility Analysis

1. Gemini Man & Aries Woman

Compatibility: High

Dynamics: Both are energetic and adventurous, making for a lively and stimulating relationship. Aries' boldness complements Gemini's curiosity.

Challenges: Aries' impulsiveness may clash with Gemini's variable moods. Mutual understanding is needed to balance independence and activity.

2. Gemini Man & Taurus Woman

Compatibility: Moderate

Dynamics: Taurus' steadiness contrasts with Gemini's restless nature. They can learn from each other—Taurus providing stability, Gemini adding variety.

Challenges: Taurus may find Gemini's flirtatiousness superficial, while Gemini might view Taurus as too possessive or slow.

3. Gemini Man & Gemini Woman

Compatibility: Very High

Dynamics: Both are talkative, curious, and adaptable, sharing intellectual pursuits and social interests.

Challenges: Possible boredom or superficiality. Communication must deepen for long-term harmony.

4. Gemini Man & Cancer Woman

Compatibility: Moderate

Dynamics: Cancer offers emotional depth, while Gemini provides mental stimulation. They can learn from each other's differences.

Challenges: Cancer's emotional sensitivity may be overwhelmed by Gemini's flirtatious or inconsistent behavior.

5. Gemini Man & Leo Woman

Compatibility: High

Dynamics: Both love socializing, adventure, and intellectual engagement. Their relationship can be lively and fun.

Challenges: Leo's need for attention may clash with Gemini's desire for variety. Mutual appreciation is essential.

6. Gemini Man & Virgo Woman

Compatibility: Moderate

Dynamics: Virgo's practicality balances Gemini's spontaneity; both can enjoy intellectual pursuits.

Challenges: Virgo's critical nature may frustrate Gemini's free-spirited side. Patience is needed.

7. Gemini Man & Libra Woman

Compatibility: Very High

Dynamics: Both are social, charming, and love intellectual conversations. They enjoy a harmonious and balanced partnership.

Challenges: Both can be indecisive; they should work together to make firm decisions.

8. Gemini Man & Scorpio Woman

Compatibility: Low to Moderate

Dynamics: Scorpio's emotional depth contrasts with Gemini's lightheartedness, which can create tension.

Challenges: Scorpio craves emotional intensity; Gemini prefers mental stimulation. Setting clear emotional boundaries is key.

9. Gemini Man & Sagittarius Woman

Compatibility: Very High

Dynamics: Both love adventure, exploration, and freedom. Their relationship is dynamic, exciting, and inspiring.

Challenges: Both highly value independence; maintaining emotional intimacy and commitment may require effort.

10. Gemini Man & Capricorn Woman

Compatibility: Moderate

Dynamics: Capricorn's discipline complements Gemini's adaptability, offering growth through contrast.

Challenges: Capricorn's seriousness may clash with Gemini's playful nature. Mutual patience is essential.

11. Gemini Man & Aquarius Woman

Compatibility: Very High

Dynamics: Both are intellectual, innovative, and value personal freedom. Their bond is often stimulating and forward-thinking.

Challenges: Both need independence; ensuring a strong emotional connection is important.

12. Gemini Man & Pisces Woman

Compatibility: Moderate

Dynamics: Pisces' emotional depth contrasts with Gemini's mental focus, creating an intriguing balance.

Challenges: Pisces may feel emotionally unfulfilled by Gemini's detachment. Clear, compassionate communication helps bridge the gap.

Aries: A Gemini woman and Aries man share an energetic and adventurous connection. Both are spontaneous, love excitement, and enjoy new experiences, leading to a lively and stimulating relationship. Their mutual enthusiasm can create strong chemistry, though they must balance impulsiveness with patience to avoid conflicts.

Taurus: Taurus and Gemini have contrasting tendencies—Taurus values stability and routine, while Gemini craves variety and novelty. While Gemini's lightheartedness can bring cheer to Taurus, maintaining deep emotional security might be challenging. Open communication and flexibility are key for their compatibility to flourish.

Gemini: Two Geminis together likely share an intensely engaging and communicative bond. Their mutual curiosity and love for intellectual stimulation ensure a relationship filled with lively conversations and shared adventures. However, they should be mindful of their tendency toward inconsistency and superficiality in order to grow deeply.

Cancer: A Gemini woman and Cancer man may experience a mix of contrasting needs—Cancer seeks emotional depth and security, while Gemini is more intellectual and social. Building trust and understanding emotional cues are vital for their harmony, as they can complement each other through a balance of heart and mind.

Leo: Leo and Gemini can have a dazzling and dynamic partnership. Both enjoy socializing, fun, and expressing themselves, making them highly compatible for lively activities and creative pursuits. Their shared enthusiasm fosters mutual admiration, and their playful natures keep the relationship vibrant.

Virgo: Virgo tends to appreciate order and practicality, which may contrast with Gemini's spontaneous and sometimes scatterbrained nature. However, their shared love for learning and intellectual pursuits can create a stimulating mental connection. To succeed, they need to appreciate each other's differing approaches.

Libra: A Gemini woman and Libra man are ideal matches for harmonious and balanced interactions. Both are social, love art and culture, and thrive on intellectual exchanges. Their relationship is likely to be affectionate and cooperative, with mutual appreciation and shared interests serving as strong foundations.

Scorpio: Scorpio's intense and passionate nature can be challenging for the breezy and light-hearted Gemini. While Scorpio seeks deep emotional bonds and loyalty, Gemini's flirtatious and changeable tendencies might be misunderstood. Patience and honesty are essential for emotional understanding.

Sagittarius: Sagittarius and Gemini are both adventurous, free-spirited, and love exploring new ideas and places. Their shared zest for life makes for an exciting, fun-filled partnership. Freedom and mutual respect for independence are crucial to avoid feelings of confinement.

Capricorn: Capricorn's disciplined and goal-oriented demeanor may seem at odds with Gemini's spontaneous nature. However, Gemini can bring a sense of fun and lightness that balances Capricorn's seriousness. They can complement each other with effort, blending stability and adaptability.

Aquarius: Aquarius and Gemini are highly compatible, both being air signs with a love for innovation and intellectual conversation. Their relationship is often based on friendship, shared ideals, and mutual respect, making it mentally stimulating and progressive.

Pisces: Pisces offers emotional depth and sensitivity, which can provide grounding for the more playful and curious Gemini woman. While their approaches to life differ, their mutual empathy can foster a caring connection, with Gemini offering a sense of lightness and Pisces providing emotional insight.

Cancer: Ruled by the moon and a water sign, represents the Crab.

Chapter 6

Cancer: (June 21- July 22)

Male Traits: protective, intuitive, and influenced by the moon.

What its's like dating a Cancer man? Cancer men are highly attuned to their feeling and the emotions of those around them. They can be deeply caring and empathetic partners, but also take things to heart easily. They are loyal and committed, once a Cancer man decides to commit, he is incredibly loyal and will go to great lengths to support and protect his partner. He values long-term relationships and stability. Cancer men are often nurturing and love to take care of their partners, creating a comforting and loving atmosphere. They enjoy making their loved ones feel secure and appreciated. They can read emotions well and often sense when something is off. This intuition makes them great listeners, as they can provide valuable support when needed.

Cancer men typically value family and home life. They may enjoy cozy nights in, family gatherings, and nurturing their domestic space, so they often see partners who share similar values about home and family. Cancer men can be very protective of their loved ones and may sometimes appear possessive. They want to ensure the people they care about feel safe and secure in the relationship.

How to get a Cancer man to fall in love with you?

Show your emotional side. Be open about your feelings and encourage him to share his. He appreciates depth in conversations and seeks a partner who is emotionally aware and willing to connect on a deeper level. Make him feel comfortable and secure in the relationship. Show affection and support through little gestures that demonstrate you care about his feelings and well-being. Understand that your cancer man may retreat or become moody at times, so be patient and give him space when needed, offering support without pressure. Bond over shared experiences that allow for emotional connections like cooking together, watching movies at home, or spending time with family.

Make sure you show love and appreciation through words and actions. Cuddling him and heartfelt gestures resonate with cancer men, It makes them feel cherished. Authenticity is important to Cancer men, so be sincere in your feelings and intentions to build trust and security in the relationship. Support his aspirations and goals and help him feel valued for his dreams and ambitions, by understanding the nurturing and sensitive nature of a Cancer man can create an environment filled with security, love, and emotional depth that can foster a meaningful connection and may lead to a lasting, loving relationship.

Female Traits: nurturing, emotional, home-oriented Influence by the Moon.

What it's like dating a Cancer woman? Dating a cancer women can be a nurturing, deeply emotional experience. Cancer women bring a lot of warmth and affection to their relationships, they are like cancer men, highly intuitive, and tend to pick up on the feelings of those around them. Her nurturing side often has her enjoying taking care of her loved ones. She thrives best where there is mutual support and care. Once she commits, a cancer woman is fiercely loyal. She values long-term relationships and seeks stability in love. She can be sensitive and may take things personally, so try to be easy on her feelings, she can easily be hurt if she feels unappreciated or neglected.

How to get a Cancer woman to fall in love with you?

Be open about your feelings and encourage her to express herself. Cancer women appreciate emotional honesty and vulnerability. Foster a nurturing environment where she feels secure and comfortable expressing her emotions, your support and understanding will mean a lot to her. Share her values about family and home life. Show that you're interested in building a future that includes family connections. Recognize that she may have mood swings and approach these instances with patience and empathy, allowing her space without pressure. By being sensitive and protective towards you, a cancer woman will create a definite loyal partner.

Cancer- The Crab

The Crab's hard shell protects its inner body, representing sensitivity. Cancer individuals often have a tough exterior while being sensitive and nurturing on the inside. Just like a Crab is protective of it's habitat and young, Cancer individuals are often seen as protectors of their loved ones and tend to be very loyal.

The parts of the body Cancer is associated with are the stomach, the breast, and the chest. Foods such as Oatmeal, melons, bananas, green vegetables, and yogurts are a good source for the Crab.

Compatibility Analysis

1. Cancer Man & Aries Woman

Compatibility Level: Moderate to Good

Dynamics: The fiery Aries can energize the sensitive Cancer, bringing excitement. Cancer offers emotional security to Aries, while Aries brings enthusiasm.

Challenges: Aries' impulsiveness might clash with Cancer's need for emotional depth and security. Patience and understanding are key.

Potential: If they align their energies, this duo can balance each other—Cancer's nurturing can calm Aries' fiery spirit.

2. Cancer Man & Taurus Woman

Compatibility Level: Excellent

Dynamics: Both are ruled by the Moon and Venus, emphasizing emotional connection, stability, and sensuality.
Strengths: Deep mutual understanding, shared values, and a love for comfort and security.

Potential: A strong, enduring bond with emotional and material harmony—making this one of the best matches.

3. Cancer Man & Gemini Woman

Compatibility Level: Moderate

Dynamics: Gemini's love for variety may challenge Cancer's need for emotional consistency. Cancer seeks a deep emotional connection, while Gemini is more intellectually driven.

Challenges: Communication issues and emotional misunderstandings may arise.

Potential: With effort, they can complement each other through learning and adapting—blending Cancer's depth with Gemini's versatility.

4. Cancer Man & Cancer Woman

Compatibility Level: Very High

Dynamics: Two water signs naturally understand each other's emotional depth, needs, and sensitivities.

Strengths: Mutual nurturing, empathy, and emotional intimacy foster a deeply connected relationship.

Potential: They can build a nurturing, harmonious, and long-lasting partnership.

5. Cancer Man & Leo Woman

Compatibility Level: Moderate to Good

Dynamics: Leo's outgoing, vibrant personality can complement Cancer's nurturing nature, though differences might sometimes clash.

Challenges: Leo desires admiration and attention, which Cancer might perceive as overbearing or needy.

Potential: With mutual respect, Leo's enthusiasm can energize Cancer, creating a loving and supportive dynamic.

6. Cancer Man & Virgo Woman

Compatibility Level: Excellent

Dynamics: Both are caring, practical, and value stability.

Strengths: Strong mutual understanding—Virgo's attention to detail complements Cancer's emotional sensitivity.

Potential: A harmonious partnership with nurturing qualities that foster deep trust and support.

7. Cancer Man & Libra Woman

Compatibility Level: Moderate

Dynamics: Libra's love for harmony and social connections balances Cancer's emotional depth.

Challenges: Libra's indecisiveness may frustrate Cancer, and Cancer's need for intimacy might sometimes be overlooked.

Potential: A relationship that emphasizes mutual appreciation and gentle understanding can thrive.

8. Cancer Man & Scorpio Woman

Compatibility Level: Very High

Dynamics: Both water signs share emotional intensity, depth, and loyalty.

Strengths: Deep connection, mutual understanding, and emotional security.

Potential: A passionate, enduring, and deeply bonding relationship.

9. Cancer Man & Sagittarius Woman

Compatibility Level: Moderate

Dynamics: Sagittarius' love for adventure may conflict with Cancer's need for stability.

Challenges: Freedom and exploration versus emotional security.

Potential: If they find common ground, Sagittarius can bring optimism to Cancer's emotional life.

10. Cancer Man & Capricorn Woman

Compatibility Level: Very Good

Dynamics: Both are cardinal signs focused on goals—Cancer on emotional well-being, Capricorn on achievement.

Strengths: They balance each other's strengths: Cancer provides emotional warmth, Capricorn offers structure.

Potential: A stable, nurturing, and ambitious partnership.

11. Cancer Man & Aquarius Woman

Compatibility Level: Moderate

Dynamics: Aquarius' love for independence contrasts with Cancer's emotional need for closeness.

Challenges: Emotional needs and social lifestyles may differ.

Potential: Through understanding and patience, they can learn from each other's differences.

12. Cancer Man & Pisces Woman

Compatibility Level: Very High

Dynamics: Both are water signs—highly intuitive, empathetic, and emotionally driven.

Strengths: Deep emotional connection and mutual understanding.

Potential: An ideal match fostering a soulful, compassionate, and nurturing relationship.

Aries: A Cancer woman and Aries man can have a dynamic yet contrasting relationship. Aries' boldness may overwhelm Cancer's sensitivity, while Cancer's emotional depth may feel heavy to impulsive Aries. However, if mutual respect is nurtured, Aries can bring excitement, and Cancer can offer emotional grounding.

Taurus: This is a naturally harmonious match. Cancer's nurturing spirit pairs well with Taurus' stability and loyalty. Both value comfort, home life, and emotional security, making this relationship deeply satisfying and enduring.

Gemini: Cancer's need for emotional consistency may clash with Gemini's restless and playful nature. While Gemini offers stimulation and variety, Cancer seeks deeper emotional bonds. Patience and honest communication are key for long-term harmony.

Cancer: Two Cancers together can create a profoundly nurturing and empathetic relationship. They intuitively understand each other's moods and emotional needs. While this can be comforting, it can also lead to emotional overload if not balanced with outside perspective.

Leo: Cancer may feel neglected by Leo's need for attention, while Leo might find Cancer too clingy or emotional. However, if they learn to appreciate their differences, Leo's warmth and Cancer's care can create a passionate, protective union.

Virgo: Cancer and Virgo form a quietly strong bond based on mutual loyalty, practicality, and care. Virgo's grounded nature helps stabilize Cancer's emotions, while Cancer brings warmth to Virgo's reserved demeanor, making for a nurturing, balanced relationship.

Libra: Libra's sociable and charming personality can attract Cancer, but Cancer's emotional depth may be overlooked in Libra's pursuit of harmony. They must bridge emotional expression and intellectual detachment to maintain balance and intimacy.

Scorpio: This is a deeply emotional and magnetic match. Both signs value loyalty, intensity, and trust, creating a strong bond. While occasional jealousy may arise, their shared intuition and emotional depth often lead to profound understanding and devotion.

Sagittarius: Cancer seeks closeness and emotional bonding, while Sagittarius thrives on freedom and exploration. Their differences can cause friction, but if they find mutual respect, Sagittarius can inspire growth, and Cancer can offer emotional depth.

Capricorn: This pairing blends emotional strength with practical ambition. Cancer nurtures the home and emotional life, while Capricorn secures the future materially and structurally. Together, they form a supportive and goal-oriented partnership.

Aquarius: Cancer may feel emotionally unfulfilled by Aquarius' detached, independent nature. Aquarius values freedom and innovation, while Cancer craves intimacy. If they embrace their differences, Aquarius can help Cancer broaden her horizons, and Cancer can ground Aquarius emotionally.

Pisces: This is a soulful, dreamy, and highly intuitive pairing. Both are deeply emotional, empathetic, and romantic, often forming a psychic connection. Their mutual understanding fosters a nurturing and spiritually rich relationship.

Leo: Ruled by the Sun, and a fire sign, represents the Lion.

Chapter 7

Leo: (July 23- August 22)

Male Traits: charismatic, confident, theatrical, influenced by the Sun.

What it's like to date a Leo man? Leo men have a magnetic and vibrant personality. They thrive in social settings and often enjoy being the star of the show. Their dynamic nature can make dating an exciting adventure. Leos carry themselves with an air of confidence. They know what they want and aren't afraid to go after it. This self- assuredness can be attractive but may also come off as a bit overwhelming at times. Leo men are known for their generous spirits. They love to spoil their partners with romantic gestures, gifts, and affection, making their loved ones feel special and valued. When they're into someone, they bring a lot of passion to the relationship. A Leo man loves deeply and expresses his feelings vividly, often displaying a fiery yet loving nature. Leo men enjoy activities that allow them to express themselves. They see our excitement; whether it's trying new things or going on adventurous dates. They have a strong sense of pride and often desire to be admired and respected by their partner. Compliments and appreciation can go a long way in making a Leo man feel loved.

How to get a Leo man to fall in love with you?

Winning a heart of a Leo man can be an exciting journey, as they are known for their loyalty and charisma. Leo men thrive on admiration and acknowledgment. Compliment him sincerely on his looks, achievements, and talents. Let him know what you admire about him, as this will boost his confidence and make him feel valued. Leos are drawn to confident individuals who can stand on their own. Showcase your self-assurance and independence in social situations. This will not only attract him but also spark his interest, as he appreciates partners who have their own lives and passions. Being open and honest about your feelings can strengthen your connection with a Leo man. They appreciate authenticity and vulnerability, so don't hold back, let him know how you feel in an empowering way. Show support by being his biggest cheerleader. Support his aspirations and celebrate his successes. A Leo man values loyalty and a partner who encourages him to pursue his dreams. Leo men tend to enjoy romance, so don't hesitate to introduce thoughtful gestures. Plan candlelit dinners, surprise him with thoughtful gifts, or just write him a sweet note. These romantic gestures go a long way. Allow him space and freedom to pursue his interest and friendships without him feeling smothered. Leo men easily detect insincerity, so be yourself and avoid trying to impress him with things that aren't true to who you are. He respects real connections to build on honesty.

Leos love excitement! Introduce an element of adventure into your interactions, whether it's planning unexpected outings, trying new experiences, or incorporating spontaneity into your time together. By utilizing these strategies, you can foster a connection with a Leo man with the chances of making him fall in love with you.

Female traits: regal, creative, passionate influenced by the Sun.

What's it like to date a Leo woman? Dating a Leo woman can be a vibrant and passionate experience. Known for their warmth, charisma, and fierce loyalty, Leo women bring a lot of energy into their relationships. Leo women exude confidence and have a strong sense of self.

They know what they want in life and love, and appreciate partners who recognize and respect her independence. When a Leo woman loves, she does so wholeheartedly and passionately. She enjoys romance and grand gestures, and she's likely to express her feelings openly. Leo women are generous with their affection. They love to spoil their partners and make them feel special.

This could be through thoughtful surprises, gifts, or simply by showering you with attention. They appreciate spontaneity and new experiences, so be prepared for travel and adventures together. Once feeling secure, they commit and are fiercely loyal. She will stand and defend you making her a dependable partner, while also expecting loyalty and respect in return.

How to get a Leo woman to fall in love with you?

Leo women love admiration and attention. Compliment her sincerely on her achievements, looks, and personality. Show her you appreciate her uniqueness and strengths. Confidence is attractive to a Leo woman. Be self-assured, express your opinions, and don't be overly submissive. She wants a partner to match her energy. Make grand romantic gestures, but also remember the small details. Plan surprise dates, give her thoughtful gifts, and show her that you deeply care. Leo women often enjoy discussing interests and passions. Share yours with her and listen to hers with enthusiasm. By understanding the traits that define a Leo woman's authenticity and spirit, you can create a strong, loving connection that may lead to lasting romance.

Leo- The Lion

Lions are often seen as powerful creatures, embodying strength and bravery. Leos are often natural leaders, the lions position as king of the jungle reflects its leadership qualities. The lion is also linked to creativity and just as lions are majestic and regal, they often have a flair for drama and enjoy being in the spotlight. Overall, the regal, vibrant, and dynamic qualities of the Leo embodies the spirit and leadership of the Lion.

The parts of the body that the Lion is associated with are the heart, the spine, and the upper back. Foods such as all lean proteins, grains, beans, and leafy greens are a good source for the Lion.

Compatibility Analysis

1. Leo Man & Aries Woman

Compatibility: High

Dynamics: Both are fire signs with strong personalities, making their relationship vibrant and passionate. They enjoy adventure, challenge, and share mutual respect for each other's strength and independence.

Challenges: Aries's impulsiveness may clash with Leo's desire for admiration and control. Balancing independence with teamwork is essential.

2. Leo Man & Taurus Woman

Compatibility: Moderate

Dynamics: Taurus offers grounding and sensuality, while Leo brings excitement and charm. Their differences can complement each other, creating a stable yet lively bond.

Challenges: Taurus's stubbornness and Leo's need for attention may create power struggles. Patience and compromise are vital.

3. Leo Man & Gemini Woman

Compatibility: High

Dynamics: Both are social, fun-loving, and full of life. Gemini's curiosity and wit match well with Leo's charisma and warmth, making this a dynamic and engaging pairing.

Challenges: Gemini's changeability and Leo's pride may cause temporary disconnects. Open, honest communication helps maintain balance.

4. Leo Man & Cancer Woman

Compatibility: Moderate

Dynamics: Cancer's emotional depth can soften Leo's boldness, while Leo offers warmth and protection. Together, they can form a caring and loyal partnership.

Challenges: Cancer's sensitivity and Leo's need for attention may cause misunderstandings. Emotional patience and empathy are needed.

5. Leo Man & Leo Woman

Compatibility: Moderate to High

Dynamics: Two Leos together create a passionate, creative, and attention-grabbing pair. They understand each other's need to shine and thrive in the spotlight.

Challenges: Competition and ego clashes may arise. Mutual admiration and taking turns in the spotlight help maintain harmony.

6. Leo Man & Virgo Woman

Compatibility: Moderate

Dynamics: Virgo's practicality and thoughtfulness balance Leo's flair and enthusiasm. Leo can help Virgo loosen up, while Virgo keeps Leo grounded.

Challenges: Virgo's critical nature may wound Leo's pride. Constructive communication and mutual appreciation are essential.

7. Leo Man & Libra Woman

Compatibility: High

Dynamics: Both enjoy romance, beauty, and socializing. Libra's diplomacy complements Leo's confidence, creating a relationship filled with grace and charm.

Challenges: Both enjoy attention, so managing ego and sharing the spotlight is necessary for long-term success.

8. Leo Man & Scorpio Woman

Compatibility: Moderate

Dynamics: Scorpio's depth and intensity can match Leo's passion and power. They're both strong-willed and devoted, creating a relationship full of fire and emotion.

Challenges: Power struggles and jealousy can surface. Trust, honesty, and emotional balance are crucial.

9. Leo Man & Sagittarius Woman

Compatibility: Very High

Dynamics: Both are adventurous, optimistic, and love excitement. Their relationship is filled with fun, spontaneity, and shared enthusiasm for life.

Challenges: They may need to make space for emotional depth and not just focus on excitement. A little grounding enhances the bond.

10. Leo Man & Capricorn Woman

Compatibility: Moderate

Dynamics: Capricorn's ambition and structure blend with Leo's creativity and warmth. They can form a strong team, each bringing different strengths to the table.

Challenges: Differences in emotional expression and lifestyle may cause friction. Mutual respect is vital.

11. Leo Man & Aquarius Woman

Compatibility: High

Dynamics: Aquarius's independence and intellect pair well with Leo's passion and flair. Together, they challenge and inspire one another.

Challenges: Emotional connection may need nurturing, as both value freedom. Understanding and flexibility are key.

12. Leo Man & Pisces Woman

Compatibility: Moderate

Dynamics: Pisces's empathy and softness can balance Leo's bold and expressive nature. Leo, in turn, gives Pisces protection and confidence.

Challenges: Emotional misalignment and different priorities may arise. Compassion and patience strengthen the bond.

Aries: A Leo woman and Aries man share a passionate and energetic connection. Both are fiery signs, which fuels mutual enthusiasm and adventure. Their relationship is marked by confidence, spontaneity, and a strong desire for excitement. While they understand each other's need for independence and leadership, they can also experience rivalry if not balanced carefully. When harmonized, their bond is vibrant and inspiring.

Taurus: Leo woman and Taurus man can create a contrasting yet complementary partnership. The Leo's fiery enthusiasm and flair for the dramatic blend well with Taurus's grounded and sensual nature. Taurus brings stability and patience to Leo's exuberance, fostering security. However, disagreements may arise from Taurus's stubbornness and Leo's need for recognition. Patience and mutual appreciation are key to long-term harmony.

Gemini: This pairing often enjoys lively conversation, shared humor, and a mutual love for social activities. The Leo woman's charisma draws in the curious and versatile Gemini man, who appreciates her warmth and leadership qualities. Both value independence, yet their relationship can sometimes lack depth if not nurtured carefully. Their mutual adaptability and zest for life help keep the relationship dynamic.

Cancer: The Leo woman and Cancer man may face challenges due to differing emotional needs—Leo seeks admiration and excitement, while Cancer craves nurturing and emotional security. However, if they work on understanding each other, Leo can provide Cancer with confidence and encouragement, while Cancer offers emotional depth. Their relationship has the potential for loyalty and genuine affection if balanced carefully.

Leo: Two Leos together can create a very regal and passionate relationship filled with mutual admiration, high energy, and shared ambitions. They understand each other's need for recognition and enjoy being the center of attention together. While their similar personalities can lead to clashes over pride or control, their common goals and enthusiasm often help them build a powerful partnership.

Virgo: The pragmatic and detail-oriented Virgo may find Leo's flamboyance and desire for attention a bit overwhelming at times. However, Virgo's dedication and practicality can help ground Leo's fiery nature. The key is for Leo to appreciate Virgo's support and attention to detail, while Virgo can learn to embrace spontaneity and express admiration more openly.

Libra: The Leo woman and Libra man often enjoy a harmonious and romantically balanced relationship. Both value social settings, beauty, and harmony, which fosters mutual understanding. Libra's diplomatic nature complements Leo's boldness, and together, they create a charming and affectionate partnership. However, Libra's indecisiveness can sometimes challenge Leo's assertiveness.

Scorpio: This might be one of the most intense and passionate matches. Leo's exuberance and Scorpio's depth create a fiery and magnetic connection. Both signs crave loyalty, passion, and emotional intensity, making their bond powerful and transformative. They can face challenges related to control and jealousy, but with mutual understanding, their relationship can be deeply fulfilling.

Sagittarius: Both signs share a love for adventure, freedom, and exploration, making them highly compatible. Leo's enthusiasm and Sagittarian optimism promote a lively, spontaneous relationship filled with travel and new experiences. Their mutual independence is appreciated, though they must ensure they remain emotionally connected rather than just thrill-seeking partners.

Capricorn: The practical and disciplined Capricorn may find Leo's flamboyance and desire for attention less compatible with their serious demeanor. Nevertheless, Leo can bring warmth and excitement into Capricorn's life, while Capricorn provides stability and focus. Success depends on mutual respect and the willingness to bridge their contrasting energies.

Aquarius: These two signs connect on an intellectual level, inspiring innovative ideas and social activism. Leo's creativity and desire for recognition blend well with Aquarius's originality and independence. Their relationship can thrive on friendship and shared ideals, though they should be mindful of emotional expression to maintain closeness.

Pisces: The gentle and dreamy Pisces may provide the emotional softness that Leo craves, while Leo's confidence can help bring Pisces out of their shell. Their relationship is characterized by compassion and mutual understanding. However, Pisces's escapism could sometimes clash with Leo's desire for admiration and recognition, requiring patience and open communication to thrive.

Virgo: Ruled by Mercury, and an earth sign, represents the Virgin.

Chapter 8

Virgo: (August 23 – September 22)

Male traits: Analytical, meticulous, practical Influence of Mercury.

What it's like to date a Virgo man? Dating a Virgo man can be a rewarding experience characterized by intelligence, practicality, and a strong sense of loyalty. Virgo men are highly analytical and detail-oriented. They tend to observe their environment carefully and evaluate situations before acting, which can sometimes come across as reserved or critical. Virgo men are practical and often approach life with a realistic mindset. They value stability and routine, and they appreciate partners who share similar values. Once a Virgo man commits to a relationship, he is incredibly loyal and dedicated. He often shows love and affection through acts of service, helping and supporting his partner. Virgo men often take their time in expressing their feelings. They might appear shy or withdrawn at first, as they tend to be cautious about opening up emotionally. They often set high standards for themselves and others, which may manifest as a desire for order. This perfectionism can be admirable, but it can also lead to self-criticism and anxiety.

How to get a Virgo Man to fall in love with you?

Virgo, I appreciate honesty and authenticity. Be yourself, and don't try to put on a facade to impress him. He values the real you. Stimulate his mind with interesting discussions, A mutual interest in topics like science, philosophy, or literature can attract him. Discuss your future plans and goals that you value while aiming towards stability and responsibility in life. Be patient with him to open up at his own pace, and don't rush him into anything, show that your willing to build trust over time. Small acts of service, like cooking his favorite meal or helping with a task, can go a long way. Virgo men often need time to themselves to recharge. Respect his personal space, and don't pressure him to spend every moment together. Be understanding of his perfectionist tendencies and avoid criticizing him for wanting things a certain way. Virgo men often have clear aspirations and ambitions, and while Virgo men may not be overly expressive initially, they do appreciate affection. Be warm and nurturing in your gestures, showing him that he is valued and loved. By understanding these traits that define a Virgo man, you can create a strong bond that has the potential to flourish into a loving and lasting relationship.

What's it like to date a Virgo woman? Dating a Virgo woman can be a delightful and enriching experience. Virgo women can make a relationship both fulfilling and enjoyable. Virgo women have a keen eye for detail and enjoy intellectual discussions. You can expect to have engaging conversations that challenge your thoughts and ideas. Virgo women appreciate stability, so they are often responsible and organized. They genuinely care about their loved ones and often express their affection through acts of service and support. Once a Virgo woman chooses to commit, she is incredibly loyal. She will work hard to maintain a healthy relationship. She doesn't always wear her heart on her sleeve, which can make it challenging at times to understand her feelings. However, once she trusts you, she will open up emotionally.

How to get a Virgo woman to fall in love with you?

Virgo women value honesty and authenticity. Be true to yourself and avoid trying to impress her with a facade. She appreciates deep connections based on trust. Stimulate her mind with conversations that flow and are meaningful. Virgo women are attracted more to kindness and empathy. Show her you care, and not just through words but actions. Understand she may take her time to express her emotions, so allow her to open up at her own pace and create a safe space for her feelings without pushing her. Show that you can be grounded and practical too. Virgo women love partners who have a clear sense of direction in life. Show genuine interest in her goals and help her achieve them, whether through emotional support or practical assistance. Demonstrating reliability and stability can win her trust in knowing you can be counted on through good times and challenges. By understanding the traits unique to a Virgo woman while building a strong foundation of trust, respect, and affection, you can create a connection that deepens over time, ultimately leading her to fall in love with you.

Virgo- The Virgin

The Virgin represents modesty, and a nurturing spirit. The Virgin represents not just a physical aspect of purity, but an intellectual and spiritual clarity, reflecting Virgo's analytical and meticulous nature. This sign is often linked with their desire to help others and improve their surroundings. The Virgin archetype embodies a sense of wholeness and the ability to discern what is essential, representing a balance of earthly and divine daily life.

The parts of the body that the Virgin is associated with are the nervous system, digestive system, and the skin. Foods such as whole grains, avocados, antioxidants like berries and teas are a good source for the Virgin.

Compatibility Analysis

1. Virgo Man & Aries Woman

Compatibility: Moderate

Details: Aries women bring passion and spontaneity, which can excite the Virgo man. However, Virgo's need for order and detailed planning may clash with Aries' impulsiveness. Communication and patience are key to balancing their differences.

2. Virgo Man & Taurus Woman

Compatibility: High

Details: Both earth signs, they share values like stability, loyalty, and practicality. Their bond is grounded, with mutual understanding and a love for routine, making for a harmonious partnership.

3. Virgo Man & Gemini Woman

Compatibility: Moderate to Good

Details: Gemini women are curious and lively, which can complement Virgo's analytical nature. The challenge is Virgo's tendency to worry and overthink, which might clash with Gemini's versatility and need for variety.

4. Virgo Man & Cancer Woman

Compatibility: Very High

Details: Both signs are caring and nurturing, valuing emotional security. Their shared sensitivity fosters a deep, supportive connection, with Virgo offering practicality and Cancer bringing emotional depth.

5. Virgo Man & Leo Woman

Compatibility: Moderate

Details: Leo women are outgoing and crave attention, while Virgo men are more reserved and detail-oriented. Their differences can either create complementarity or friction, requiring effort to understand each other's worlds.

6. Virgo Man & Virgo Woman

Compatibility: Excellent

Details: Both are perfectionists and detail-focused, sharing a strong understanding of each other's routines and values. Their relationship is likely to be stable and harmonious, with shared goals.

7. Virgo Man & Libra Woman

Compatibility: Good

Details: Libra's charm and social nature can complement Virgo's practicality. Balancing Virgo's need for order with Libra's love of harmony and aesthetics is essential for lasting harmony.

8. Virgo Man & Scorpio Woman

Compatibility: Very High

Details: Both signs are intense and value loyalty. Virgo's grounded nature pairs well with Scorpio's emotional depth, creating a relationship built on trust, understanding, and shared purpose.

9. Virgo Man & Sagittarius Woman

Compatibility: Moderate

Details: Sagittarius' love for adventure contrasts with Virgo's preference for routine. They can learn from each other—Virgo offers stability, while Sagittarius brings energy and excitement.

10. Virgo Man & Capricorn Woman

Compatibility: Very High

Details: Both are ambitious, practical, and value stability. Their relationship can be deeply supportive, with shared goals and strong mutual respect.

11. Virgo Man & Aquarius Woman

Compatibility: Moderate

Details: Aquarius' innovative and unconventional approach may challenge Virgo's need for order. However, their shared intellect can lead to stimulating conversations if differences are managed.

12. Virgo Man & Pisces Woman

Compatibility: Good

Details: Pisces' dreaminess and emotional sensitivity can soften Virgo's pragmatic nature. They may form a loving, compassionate partnership, enriching each other's worlds.

Aries: A Virgo woman and Aries man can create a dynamic duo, balancing Virgo's meticulousness with Aries' adventurous spirit. While Aries brings excitement and spontaneity, Virgo offers stability and attention to detail, fostering growth through mutual understanding. However, Aries' impulsiveness might occasionally clash with Virgo's cautious nature, requiring patience and open communication for harmony.

Taurus: Virgo and Taurus share earth element qualities, resulting in a grounded, dependable relationship. Both appreciate stability, loyalty, and practical values, which helps them build a secure foundation. Their shared love for routine and comfort fosters trust, but they should ensure they allow space for spontaneity to keep their bond vibrant.

Gemini: Virgo and Gemini are different in many ways—Virgo's methodical approach contrasts with Gemini's lively, curious nature. While Virgo's practicality can complement Gemini's adaptability, their differences might cause misunderstandings. Open-mindedness and patience are key for these two to connect intellectually and emotionally.

Cancer: Virgo and Cancer often find a natural affinity, as both signs are nurturing and value emotional security. Virgo's attention to detail supports Cancer's sensitive nature, creating a caring environment. Their shared goals of stability and family can deepen their bond, although Virgo's critical tendencies may need to be tempered to avoid hurting Cancer's feelings.

Leo: Virgo and Leo may face challenges due to their contrasting energies—Virgo's modesty contrasts with Leo's love of attention. However, Virgo's practicality can ground Leo's flamboyance, and Leo can inspire Virgo to step out of their comfort zone. Respecting each other's differences fosters growth and appreciation.

Virgo: Two Virgos together can build a harmonious, detail-oriented partnership. Their shared values for order, cleanliness, and responsibility make for a stable relationship. However, their perfectionism might lead to overcritical tendencies, so mutual understanding is essential to nurture compassion.

Libra: Virgo and Libra can complement each other well, balancing Virgo's practicality with Libra's love of harmony and aesthetics. While Virgo may focus on details and analysis, Libra's social grace can help smooth their interactions. Their different decision-making styles require compromise for a harmonious union.

Scorpio: Virgo and Scorpio can form a deep, intense connection. Virgo's analytical mind and Scorpio's emotional depth complement each other, fostering trust and loyalty. Both are committed and focused, but Virgo's need for order may sometimes conflict with Scorpio's intensity, requiring patience and understanding.

Sagittarius: Virgo and Sagittarius have contrasting approaches—Virgo's meticulousness versus Sagittarius's love of freedom and adventure. While their differences can challenge their compatibility, mutual respect can help them learn from each other. Virgo can teach Sagittarius about responsibility, while Sagittarius can encourage Virgo to explore beyond their routines.

Capricorn: As fellow earth signs, Virgo and Capricorn are highly compatible, sharing ambitions, discipline, and practicality. Their mutual respect for work ethic and stability fosters a resilient relationship. Together, they can achieve long-term goals, supporting each other's growth and success.

Aquarius: Virgo and Aquarius bring different energies to the table—Virgo's practicality versus Aquarius's innovative and unconventional ideas. While this can be a stimulating pairing, it may also lead to misunderstandings if not managed carefully. Open-mindedness and shared values can bridge their differences for a balanced partnership.

Pisces: Virgo and Pisces can create a compassionate, supportive relationship. Virgo's grounded nature complements Pisces's dreamy tendencies, providing stability to their emotional worlds. Their mutual sensitivity fosters deep understanding, but Virgo's critical side may require conscious effort to avoid unintentionally hurting.

Libra: Ruled by Venus, and an air sign, represents the scale.

Chapter 9

Libra: (September 23 – October 22)

Male traits: Diplomatic, social, romantic influence of the scale.

What's it like to date a Libra man? Dating a Libra man can be an exciting and harmonious experience. Known for their charm, diplomacy, and love for beauty and balance, Libra men can bring a sense of joy and elegance into a relationship. Libra men are typically very charming and social. They have a natural ability to engage with others, making conversations enjoyable and energetic. You'll likely find him to be a great conversationalist who can make anyone feel at ease. Libra men are romantics at heart. They often have a strong sense of what love should be like and seek deep connections. Their idealism may lead them to appreciate grand romantic gestures.

Being ruled by Venus, the planet of love and beauty, Libra men seek harmony and balance in all aspects of life, including relationships. They value fairness and appreciate partners who respect their views and opinions. Libra men enjoy engaging in discussions and exploring new ideas. They often seek depth in conversations, so they appreciate partners who can stimulate their intellect. One of the challenges of dating a Libra man can be his indecisiveness. He may take time to make decisions, particularly when it comes to love or significant commitments, as he wants to weigh all options carefully.

How to get a Libra Man to fall in love with you?

Emulate the charm and friendliness that Libra men possess. Engage him in light-hearted conversations and display your social side, making him feel comfortable and appreciated. Stimulate his mind with interesting discussions.

Libra men appreciate thought-provoking topics and will be drawn to someone who can share insights and engage them on a deeper level. Show your romantic side by planning thoughtful dates or surprises. Small gestures, like leaving sweet notes or arranging a romantic dinner, can make him feel valued and adored. Since Libra men have love and beauty, show an appreciation for art, music, and aesthetics. Whether it's complimenting his style or enjoying cultural activities together, this can strengthen your bond. Be patient with his indecisions.

How to get a Libra Man to fall in love with you? Be charming and sociable. Libra men are attracted to people who are charismatic and engaging. Show your social side by being friendly, approachable, and open to meeting new people. Join him in social activities and demonstrate your ability to connect with others. Libra men are hopeless romantics at heart. Plan thoughtful dates and be expressive with your feelings. Small romantic gestures, like handwritten notes or surprise outings, will resonate with his idealistic view of love. Libra men value fairness and harmony in relationships. Show that you can navigate compromises and are willing to find middle ground. This will help build trust and mutual respect. Libra men appreciate their freedom and need for personal space. Show that you respect his independence and allow him the time he needs to focus on his interests. Understand that Libra men can be indecisive, especially when it comes to love. Be patient and avoid pressuring him into making quick decisions. Allow the relationship to develop naturally. Show that you can provide stability and companionship.

Express your values and show that you are looking for a meaningful relationship. Libra men are attracted to positive and happy individuals. Show your joyful side, and share your passions and hobbies. Your enthusiasm for life will draw him in, authenticity is the key, so be genuine in your interactions and express your true self. Libra men appreciate honesty and can easily sense when someone is being disingenuous. By being charming, engaging, and authentic while respecting his individuality, you can create a deep and meaningful connection that may lead to a loving relationship with a Libra man.

Female traits: Graceful, harmonious, loving Influence of Venus

What's it like to date a Libra woman? Dating a Libra woman can be a delightful and enriching experience. Known for their charm, grace, and sociable nature, Libra women have many characteristics that make them attractive partners. Libra women are often charming people and enjoy being around people. They thrive in social settings and have a knack for making conversations enjoyable and engaging. Libra women are naturally romantic at heart. They often have idealistic views about love and relationships and seek partners who can inspire them. They value harmony and balance in their relationships and have a strong sense of justice and fairness, and they seek to create harmonious connections with others. Libra women enjoy deep conversations and exploring perspectives which makes them drawn to those who can challenge and engage their minds. One of the challenges of dating a Libra woman is her tendency to be indecisive. She may take time to make decisions, especially when it comes to choosing activities or making commitments. Libra women place a high value on relationships and connections. They often seek to establish strong emotional ties and appreciate individuals who are willing to invest time and effort into building a relationship.

How to get a Libra woman to fall in love with you?

Libra women are attracted to charming and friendly individuals. Show off your social skills and engage her in the light, playful conversation. Be genuine and approachable, making her feel at ease. Show appreciation for aesthetics through compliments about her appearance or enjoy beautiful surroundings together. Create romantic moments that make her feel special. Surprise her with thoughtful gestures, handwritten notes, romantic dates, or small gifts. Show her that you can be a loving and attentive partner. Libra women value fairness in a relationship, and they put a high priority on a partner who can express healthy communication and compromise. Encourage social activities and be willing to meet her friends and family.

Libra women love the balance of socializing, so be participating in group activities can further and deepen your connection. Being social and friendly will help her see you as a potential partner. Plan thoughtful dates that cater to her romantic ideals. This could include candlelit dinners, surprises, or outings to beautiful locations, helping her feel cherished. Libras: Both Male and Female dislike conflict and thrive in harmonious settings. Approach disagreements calmly and diplomatically, focusing on the resolution rather than the confrontation. Keep the atmosphere light and positive. Authenticity is crucial to the Libra woman. Be genuine in your interactions and allow her to see the real you.

Libra women are drawn to individuals who are true to themselves. By understanding the qualities that attract a Libra woman and creating a connection based on mutual respect, charm, and intelligence, you can foster a loving relationship and increase the chances of her falling in love with you.

Libra- The Scale

The scale represents balance, harmony, and justice, which are key traits associated with the scale. The scale symbolizes the importance of fairness and equilibrium, suggesting that the scale requires peace and to avoid conflict in their interactions with others. The emphasis on balance also pertains to decision-making and moral judgment as Libras strive to weigh options carefully. The scale is known for its diplomatic nature, often seeking to mediate conflicts and ensure that all voices are heard.

The body parts that the scale is associated with are the kidneys, lower back, and skin.

Foods such as fatty fish, Omega 3 (Salmon, Tuna) berries, and arugula leafy greens are a good source for the scale.

Compatibility Analysis

1. Libra Man and Aries Woman

Compatibility: Moderate to Good

Dynamics: Aries brings energy and spontaneity, which can excite Libra, but Aries' impulsiveness may clash with Libra's desire for harmony. They can learn from each other—Libra's diplomacy balances Aries' assertiveness.

Strengths: Mutual admiration, adventure, and growth

Challenges: Conflict resolution, differing social needs

2. Libra Man and Taurus Woman

Compatibility: Moderate

Dynamics: Taurus provides stability and sensuality, aligning with Libra's love for beauty and harmony. However, Taurus' fixed nature can slow Libra's desire for variety.

Strengths: Romantic connection, shared appreciation for aesthetics

Challenges: Tolerance for routine, decision-making conflicts

3. Libra Man and Gemini Woman

Compatibility: Excellent

Dynamics: Both air signs, they share intellectual curiosity, communication, and social activity. Their conversations are lively and shared interests evolve naturally.

Strengths: Mental stimulation, social versatility, fun

Challenges: Potential superficiality, needing depth over time

4. Libra Man and Cancer Woman

Compatibility: Moderate

Dynamics: Cancer's emotional depth complements Libra's harmony-driven nature, but Cancer's sensitivity requires gentle handling. Libra offers balance and diplomacy.

Strengths: Emotional support, nurturing romance

Challenges: Differing needs for emotional security and independence

5. Libra Man and Leo Woman

Compatibility: Good

Dynamics: Both love beauty, socializing, and admiration, creating a lively, romantic dynamic. Leo's confidence pairs well with Libra's charm.

Strengths: Mutual admiration, celebration of love

Challenges: Pride, potential competition for attention

6. Libra Man and Virgo Woman

Compatibility: Moderate

Dynamics: Virgo's practicality and detail-oriented approach balance Libra's love for aesthetics. However, Virgo's critical tendencies may challenge Libra's peace-loving nature.

Strengths: Intellectual rapport, shared values of refinement

Challenges: Perfectionism, indecisiveness

7. Libra Man and Libra Woman

Compatibility: Excellent

Dynamics: Both value harmony, socialization, and elegance. Their relationship is characterized by mutual understanding and shared aesthetics.

Strengths: Deep compatibility, balanced partnership

Challenges: Indecisiveness, avoiding confrontations

8. Libra Man and Scorpio Woman

Compatibility: Moderate

Dynamics: Scorpio's intensity can contrast with Libra's desire for peace. But both are passionate and can learn from each other with effort.

Strengths: Deep emotional connection, loyalty

Challenges: Trust issues, power struggles

9. Libra Man and Sagittarius Woman

Compatibility: Excellent

Dynamics: Both love adventure and social activities, making their relationship vibrant and exciting. They share optimism and a love for freedom.

Strengths: Spontaneity, shared ideals

Challenges: Commitment fears, differing views on stability

10. Libra Man and Capricorn Woman

Compatibility: Moderate

Dynamics: Capricorn's ambition contrasts with Libra's focus on aesthetics and relationships. Balance can be achieved with mutual respect.

Strengths: Mutual motivation, support for ambitions

Challenges: Different social priorities

11. Libra Man and Aquarius Woman

Compatibility: Excellent

Dynamics: Both air signs, they share intellectual curiosity, humanitarian interests, and love for social engagement. Their relationship is innovative and collaborative.

Strengths: Communication, unconventional romance

Challenges: Detachment, emotional expression

12. Libra Man and Pisces Woman

Compatibility: Good

Dynamics: Pisces' emotional depth complements Libra's harmony. Their differences can create a nurturing, compassionate relationship.

Strengths: Emotional connection, mutual understanding

Challenges: Escaping reality, setting boundaries

Aries: A Libra woman and Aries man can create an exciting and dynamic partnership. Libra's tact and diplomacy balance Aries' fiery and impulsive nature, fostering mutual growth. While Aries appreciates Libra's elegance and social grace, Libra is drawn to Aries' boldness. Challenges may arise from Aries' impatience, but their differences can complement each other well if they respect each other's pace.

Taurus: Taurus and Libra often enjoy harmonious companionship rooted in a shared love for beauty, comfort, and stability. Libra's elegance and love for socializing blend seamlessly with Taurus' grounded nature and appreciation for the finer things in life. They tend to have strong mutual understanding, making their bond stable and romantic, though Taurus' possessiveness can sometimes clash with Libra's need for independence.

Gemini: The relationship between a Libra woman and a Gemini man is typically lively and intellectually stimulating. Both are air signs, which fosters excellent communication and mental connection. Libra's charm and diplomacy can complement Gemini's curiosity and adaptability. Together, they tend to have a fun, flirtatious, and engaging partnership, though they must work to keep their emotional depth alive.

Cancer: A Libra woman and Cancer man bring together air and water energies, which can create a nurturing yet intellectually stimulating bond. Libra's social grace and desire for harmony can soothe Cancer's emotional sensitivity, while Cancer's caring nature provides emotional depth. Their relationship often thrives on mutual understanding, though Cancer's need for emotional security can sometimes clash with Libra's desire for independence.

Leo: Libra and Leo often share a vibrant, socially active partnership. Libra's refined taste and love for beauty align with Leo's flair for drama and glamour. Both enjoy admiration and social outings, making their connection lively and appreciative. However, they need to be mindful of ego clashes and support each other's individuality to maintain harmony.

6. Virgo: The compatibility between a Libra woman and Virgo man can be based on mutual appreciation for beauty, harmony, and detail. Libra's diplomatic approach and Virgo's analytical mind blend well, fostering a conscientious and elegant partnership. While Virgo is practical and sometimes critical, Libra's natural charm and tact can smooth over potential misunderstandings, creating a balanced and refined relationship.

Libra: Two Libras together share a relationship rooted in harmony, romance, and mutual appreciation for aesthetics. Their partnership is often peaceful, balanced, and filled with social activities. While they may sometimes avoid confrontations, they can also struggle with decision-making due to their indecisiveness. Open communication is vital for sustaining their harmonious bond.

Scorpio: A Libra woman with a Scorpio man can be a passionate, intense pairing. Scorpio's depth and emotional strength contrast with Libra's diplomatic and social nature. This relationship can thrive if both are willing to understand and respect their differing emotional approaches. Scorpio brings depth, while Libra offers balance and grace, possibly creating a powerful, transformative connection.

Sagittarius: A Libra woman and Sagittarius man share a love for adventure, exploration, and intellectual stimulation. Both value freedom and independence, making their relationship lively and optimistic. Their shared love for new experiences can forge a strong bond, though they must remain attentive to emotional depth to avoid superficiality.

Capricorn: Capricorn and Libra can build a relationship based on mutual admiration and balance — Capricorn's ambition paired with Libra's love for harmony and social grace. While Capricorn may be more pragmatic and focused on goals, Libra brings a sense of beauty and diplomacy, helping to soften Capricorn's seriousness. Their partnership benefits from a good balance of stability and elegance.

Aquarius: A Libra woman and Aquarius man often find a deep mental and social connection. Both are air signs, favoring intellectual conversations, social activism, and independence. Their shared ideals and love for innovation can foster an inspiring relationship, though they may need to work on emotional intimacy to ensure closeness.

Pisces: A Libra woman and Pisces man appreciate romance, empathy, and emotional connection. Libra's charm and love for harmony blend well with Pisces' sensitivity and dreamy nature. Their relationship tends to be gentle, artistic, and nurturing. However, they must ensure their emotional boundaries are clear to avoid escapism or confusion.

Scorpio: Ruled by Pluto and Mars, and a water sign represents the Scorpion.

Chapter 10

Scorpio: (October 23 – November 21)

Male traits: Intense, secretive, passionate Influence of Pluto and Mars.

What's it like to date a Scorpio man? Dating a Scorpio man can be a passionate and intense experience. They're known for their depth, charisma, and emotional complexity. Scorpio men are passionate about nature. Once they commit, they tend to invest deeply in the relationship, giving their all emotionally and physically. Scorpio men often have a mysterious aura that is intriguing. They tend to keep their thoughts and emotions guarded initially, making them enigmatic. When a Scorpio man is in love, he is fiercely loyal and protective of his partner. He values trust above all else and expects the same loyalty in return. Scorpio men feel things profoundly and are not afraid to explore the darker aspects of relationships. They are highly ambitious and goal-oriented, they make it a priority to put a lot of energy into achieving their personal and professional goals. While loyalty is a virtue, Scorpio men can also be possessive. They may become jealous if they sense a threat to the relationship, so it's important to be transparent and reassuring.

How to get a Scorpio man to fall in love with you?

Be true to yourself and honest about your feelings and intentions. Authenticity is the key to building trust with a Scorpio. Engage him in meaningful conversations and share your thoughts and feelings openly. Scorpio men are private and often guard their feelings. Give him space when needed, and don't push him to open up before he's ready. Show that you respect his boundaries. While you should ultimately be genuine, keeping an air of mystery about yourself can be intriguing to your Scorpio man, so don't reveal everything about yourself too quickly, let him uncover the layers of your personality over time.

Female traits: Powerful, intuitive, transformative Influence of Pluto and Mars.

What's it like to date a Scorpio woman? Dating a Scorpio woman can be an intense and mesmerizing experience. They are known for their passionate nature. They invest deeply in their relationship and are often very committed to their partners. Their emotions run deep, and they seek meaningful connections.

Scorpio women have layers of personality that they unveil over time. This mystery can be intriguing and keeps partners engaged as they get to know her better.

They experience emotions intensely, which can lead them to be both profoundly affectionate partners who can handle the complexity of their emotions. They often have a sixth sense about people and situations, making them highly intuitive. Scorpio women can often read emotions and are attuned to their partner's needs.

How to get a Scorpio woman to fall in love with you?

Be truthful about your feelings and intentions, as they can easily spot insincerity. Show her the real you. Engage her mind, talk about subjects that intrigue her, and share thoughts openly. Open up about your experiences in life, Scorpio women often appreciate vulnerability and depth from their partners, so don't shy away from sharing that side with her. Demonstrate your commitment to her that you are trustworthy and dependable, and this may create a long fulfilling relationship with your Scorpio woman.

Scorpio- The Scorpion

The Scorpion represents Power, Control, Passion, transformation, and rebirth. Scorpions are known for their intense emotions and passionate approach to life. Just as scorpions can shed their exoskeletons, they are often seen as individuals who are capable of profound personal transformation and growth. They tend to be Mysterious often perceived as enigmatic and secretive, much like the Scorpion that tends to hide in shadows. This symbolizes their tendency to keep their true feelings and thoughts guarded. The Scorpion serves as a multifaceted symbol that captures the essence of Scorpio's emotional depth, complexity, and transformative power.

The body part that the Scorpion is associated with is the reproductive organs, particularly the genitals. Foods such as plant-based proteins, berries, Brussels sprouts, and avocado are good sources for the Scorpion.

Compatibility Analysis

1. Scorpio Man & Aries Woman

Compatibility: Moderate to High

Dynamics: The passionate Scorpio admires the Aries woman's fiery spirit and independence. Both are assertive and driven, leading to an intense connection. However, Aries' impulsiveness may sometimes clash with Scorpio's depth and need for emotional security.

Potential Challenges: Power struggles, quick tempers, jealousy.

Ideal Aspects: Mutual passion, ambition, shared desire for excitement.

2. Scorpio Man & Taurus Woman

Compatibility: Excellent

Dynamics: Both are fixed signs, creating stability and loyalty. Taurus's practicality complements Scorpio's intensity. They crave deep, lasting bonds and value loyalty.

Potential Challenges: Taurus's stubbornness versus Scorpio's control tendencies.

Ideal Aspects: Both appreciate sensuality, commitment, and trust.

3. Scorpio Man & Gemini Woman

Compatibility: Moderate

Dynamics: Gemini's social and lively nature contrasts with Scorpio's depth and seriousness. They can intrigue each other intellectually, but emotional understanding might be a hurdle.

Potential Challenges: Communication gaps, emotional misunderstandings, superficiality vs depth.

Ideal Aspects: Mutual curiosity, learning from each other.

4. Scorpio Man & Cancer Woman

Compatibility: Very High

Dynamics: Both water signs, fostering profound emotional connections. They understand each other's need for security and emotional intimacy.

Potential Challenges: Emotional overdependence if not balanced.

Ideal Aspects: Deep compassion, nurturing, loyalty.

5. Scorpio Man & Leo Woman

Compatibility: Moderate

Dynamics: Leo's charisma and love for attention can both attract and challenge Scorpio's possessiveness. They share passion but might struggle over control and recognition.

Potential Challenges: Ego clashes, jealousy.

Ideal Aspects: Mutual admiration, passion.

6. Scorpio Man & Virgo Woman

Compatibility: Moderate to High

Dynamics: Virgo's practicality balances Scorpio's intensity. Both signs value loyalty and meaningful connections.

Potential Challenges: Over-analysis, emotional restraint.

Ideal Aspects: Shared values, attention to detail, dependability.

7. Scorpio Man & Libra Woman

Compatibility: Moderate

Dynamics: Libra's charm and sociability contrast with Scorpio's depth. A relationship may require effort to balance emotional needs.

Potential Challenges: Lack of emotional depth awareness, indecision.

Ideal Aspects: Intellectual connection, mutual respect.

8. Scorpio Man & Scorpio Woman

Compatibility: Very High

Dynamics: Shared intensity and emotional depth lead to a profound bond. Both understand the need for trust and loyalty.

Potential Challenges: Possible jealousy, power struggles.

Ideal Aspects: Compatibility in passion, emotional honesty.

9. Scorpio Man & Sagittarius Woman

Compatibility: Moderate to Low

Dynamics: Sagittarius's love for adventure and freedom may clash with Scorpio's need for emotional closeness and control.

Potential Challenges: Commitment fears, differing priorities.

Ideal Aspects: Learning from each other's contrasting traits.

10. Scorpio Man & Capricorn Woman

Compatibility: High

Dynamics: Both are determined and ambitious, valuing stability and success. They can build a solid, long-term partnership.

Potential Challenges: Rigidity, work-focused attitudes.

Ideal Aspects: Mutual respect, shared goals.

11. Scorpio Man & Aquarius Woman

Compatibility: Low to Moderate

Dynamics: Aquarius's independence and unconventional thinking may challenge Scorpio's possessiveness.

Potential Challenges: Emotional disconnect, different needs.

Ideal Aspects: Opportunities for growth through differences.

12. Scorpio Man & Pisces Woman

Compatibility: Very High

Dynamics: Both water signs, fostering deep emotional understanding and empathy. They can create a spiritual and intuitive connection.

Potential Challenges: Over-sensitivity, emotional dependence.

Ideal Aspects: Compassion, emotional flow, mutual nurturing.

Aries: A Scorpio woman and Aries man can experience a passionate connection fueled by their intense personalities. While Aries' impulsiveness might challenge Scorpio's need for control, their shared enthusiasm can create exciting and dynamic interactions. Trust and patience are crucial for building a harmonious relationship.

Taurus: Scorpio and Taurus often share deep emotional bonds and similar values, making for a stable and committed partnership. Both are sensual and cherish loyalty, which fosters a nurturing environment. However, their stubborn tendencies may lead to power struggles if not managed carefully.

Gemini: A Scorpio woman and Gemini man bring contrasting energies — intensity versus versatility. While their differences can create intriguing chemistry, misunderstandings may arise due to Scorpio's need for depth and Gemini's desire for variety. Effective communication is key to their compatibility.

Cancer: Both emotional and intuitive, Scorpio and Cancer share a profound understanding of each other's feelings. This combination can result in a highly empathetic and supportive relationship, characterized by mutual trust and affection. Their shared vulnerability strengthens their bond.

Leo: A Scorpio woman and Leo man are both passionate and confident, which can lead to an exciting and fiery romance. However, their strong personalities may clash over pride and recognition. Mutual respect and openness help in balancing their relationship dynamics.

Virgo: Scorpio and Virgo connect on a practical and emotional level, appreciating each other's dedication and attention to detail. Their shared desire for stability and meaningful connection fosters a harmonious partnership, though they must remain mindful of overanalyzing.

Libra: While Libra's charm and diplomacy can soften Scorpio's intensity, their core differences — seeking harmony versus craving depth — may create challenges. Balancing Scorpio's depth with Libra's social nature requires effort but can lead to growth and mutual understanding.

Scorpio: Two Scorpios together create an intensely passionate and transformative relationship. Their shared emotional depth and loyalty can lead to an unbreakable bond, though jealousy and possessiveness require careful management to prevent conflicts.

Sagittarius: Scorpio and Sagittarius have contrasting worldviews — Scorpio's depth versus Sagittarius's love for adventure. While their differences can be stimulating, they may struggle with commitment. Open communication about expectations is vital to navigate their relationship.

Capricorn: Scorpio and Capricorn often form a powerful partnership grounded in ambition and mutual respect. Both value loyalty and stability, making them highly compatible for long-term commitment. Their combined determination can lead to shared success.

Aquarius: Scorpio and Aquarius bring different perspectives — emotional intensity versus innovative detachment. Their relationship can be intriguing but challenging, requiring both to respect each other's individuality and communicate openly to bridge their differences.

Pisces: Both intuitive and empathetic, Scorpio and Pisces tend to understand each other's emotional worlds deeply. This connection often results in a compassionate and soulful partnership, characterized by mutual support and shared dreams, though boundaries should be maintained to avoid overdependence.

Sagittarius: Ruled by Jupiter, and a fire sign, represents the Archer.

Chapter 11

Sagittarius (November 22- December 21)

Male traits: Adventurous, cheerful, outspoken Influence of Jupiter

What's it like to date a Sagittarius man? Dating a Sagittarius man can be an exhilarating and adventurous experience. Known for their optimism, adventure-seeking nature, and love for freedom, Sagittarius men bring spontaneity and excitement to relationships. A Sagittarius men love exploring new horizons, so expect exciting dates, spontaneous getaways, and a desire for new experiences. With a positive outlook on life, Sagittarius men bring joy and laughter to their relationships. They enjoy having a good time and value partners who share their sense of humor. They appreciate partners who respect their need for space and autonomy to explore their interests. Philosophical and curious, they have a deep sense of curiosity and enjoy intellectual discussions. Conversations with topics including philosophy, culture, and spirituality. With a forward–looking mindset, Sagittarius men tend to be straightforward and honest in their communication. They value transparency and appreciate partners who can communicate openly.

How to get a Sagittarius man to fall in love with you?

It's essential to appeal to his adventurous and independent nature. Sagittarius men are attracted to women who have their own goals and ambitions. Show him you are self-assured and capable of standing on your own. They are known for their love for spontaneity, so surprise him with fun and exciting activities that appeal to his thrill-seeking nature. Radiate positivity and show him that you can see the bright side of life even in challenging situations. Remember, every person is unique, so it's important to also communicate openly and honestly with

him to understand his individual preferences and interests. Good Luck!

Female traits: Free-spirited, philosophical, optimistic Influence of Jupiter.

What's it like to date a Sagittarius woman? Dating a Sagittarius woman can be an exciting and adventurous experience. These women are known for their independent and free-spirited nature.

Sagittarius women are always up for trying new things and exploring new places, so try to be open-minded. Engage her intellect, they are typically intelligent and curious individuals. Stimulate her mind with engaging discussions and a variety of topics. Sagittarius women value their freedom and independence, avoid being too clingy or controlling, and instead, give her space to pursue interests and passions. Be honest and straightforward with your feelings and intentions, as they appreciate direct communication. In essence, to capture the heart of a Sagittarius woman, you should be adventurous, intellectually stimulating, respectful of her independence, honest, and willing to embrace spontaneity.

How to get a Sagittarius woman to fall in love with you?

Show a sense of humor they enjoy a good laugh, being able to make her laugh and share light- hearted moments together can help strengthen your bond. Sagittarius women are drawn to positive individuals who can see the silver lining in any situation. Plan fun, adventurous activities to keep things interesting and cater to her love for new experiences. Respect her need for freedom and space to explore her interest. Encourage her independence and show that you are there to support her in all her endeavors. By combining these qualities and showing her that you appreciate her adventurous spirit, intelligence, humor, and independence you can capture the heart of a Sagittarius woman.

Sagittarius-The Archer

The Archer represents philosophy, freedom, adventure, and exploration. The Sagittarius is known for its love for adventure, travel, and exploration. The Archer's aim towards the quest for knowledge and new experiences embodies a positive and enthusiastic outlook on life.

Sagittarians typically like to break away from constraints and explore life on their own terms. The Archer's as a

symbol reflects the adventurous spirit, optimism, and philosophical nature of the Sagittarius.

The parts of the body that the Archer is commonly associated with are the hips, thighs, and the sciatic nerve, also linked to the liver and pelvic region. Foods such as beans for protein, sweet potatoes, kale, berries, and turmeric are good sources for the Sagittarian.

Compatibility Analysis

1. Sagittarius Man & Aries Woman

Compatibility: Highly energetic and adventurous pairing.

Strengths: Both love exploration, freedom, and spontaneity. They enjoy outdoor activities and new experiences.
Challenges: Impulsiveness can lead to conflicts if not managed well. Both need to respect independence.

Overall: A passionate, lively relationship with great potential for adventure and mutual growth.

2. Sagittarius Man & Taurus Woman

Compatibility: Good but requires effort.

Strengths: Taurus offers stability; Sagittarius brings excitement.

Challenges: Taurus's need for security may clash with Sagittarius's love for freedom. Differing priorities can cause tension.

Overall: With patience, they can balance each other — Taurus grounding Sagittarius's zest.

3. Sagittarius Man & Gemini Woman

Compatibility: Excellent.

Strengths: Both are mutable signs, love learning, and are highly social and witty.

Challenges: May lack depth if superficiality dominates.

Overall: A lively, playful match full of intellectual stimulation and fun.

4. Sagittarius Man & Cancer Woman

Compatibility: Moderate.

Strengths: Cancer offers emotional depth; Sagittarius seeks adventure.

Challenges: Cancer's emotional needs might feel neglected by Sagittarius's free spirit.

Overall: Needs effort to balance emotional closeness with independence.

5. Sagittarius Man & Leo Woman

Compatibility: Very compatible.

Strengths: Both crave adventure, enthusiasm, and independence.

Challenges: At times, their egos may clash, but mutual respect usually prevails.

Overall: A fiery, dynamic partnership full of excitement and shared passions.

6. Sagittarius Man & Virgo Woman

Compatibility: Mixed.

Strengths: Virgo offers practicality, and Sagittarius brings optimism.

Challenges: Different approaches to life — Virgo's precision vs. Sagittarius's spontaneity.

Overall: Potential exists if they appreciate each other's differences.

7. Sagittarius Man & Libra Woman

Compatibility: Very good

Strengths: Both are social, idealistic, and love beauty and ideas.

Challenges: Libra's desire for partnership and harmony may sometimes suppress Sagittarius's independence.

Overall: A charming, balanced relationship full of exploration and mutual admiration.

8. Sagittarius Man & Scorpio Woman

Compatibility: Challenging.

Strengths: Scorpio offers emotional intensity; Sagittarius loves adventure.

Challenges: Scorpio's depth may feel stifling to Sagittarius's need for freedom. Trust issues can arise.

Overall: Requires understanding and compromise to thrive.

9. Sagittarius Man & Sagittarius Woman

Compatibility: Excellent.

Strengths: Both love freedom, adventure, and honesty.

Challenges: May lack stability or depth if not mindful.

Overall: An energetic, optimistic, and fun-loving union.

10. Sagittarius Man & Capricorn Woman

Compatibility: Moderate.

Strengths: Capricorn provides structure; Sagittarius seeks spontaneity.

Challenges: Their different pacing may cause friction.

Overall: Complementary if they learn to appreciate their differences.

11. Sagittarius Man & Aquarius Woman

Compatibility: Very high.

Strengths: Both value independence, innovation, and intellectual pursuits.

Challenges: Slightly detached emotions at times, but usually compatible intellectually.

Overall: A futuristic, stimulating relationship.

12. Sagittarius Man & Pisces Woman

Compatibility: Moderate.

Strengths: Pisces offers emotional depth; Sagittarius offers adventure.

Challenges: Different emotional needs — Pisces may crave deep connection, which Sagittarius might struggle to provide.

Overall: Needs nurturing to deepen the emotional bond.

Aries: A Sagittarius woman and an Aries man often experience a dynamic and energetic connection. Both are adventurous, spontaneous, and love excitement, which fuels their relationship. They tend to share similar enthusiasm for exploring new places and ideas, making their bond lively and passionate.

However, their mutual independence can sometimes lead to conflicts over freedom and space, requiring understanding and compromise.

Taurus: Compatibility between a Sagittarius woman and Taurus man can be a bit challenging. While she seeks adventure and variety, he prefers stability and routine. This fundamental difference may cause friction unless they find a way to balance her craving for excitement with his need for security. Open communication and patience are key to fostering harmony.

Gemini: The relationship between a Sagittarius woman and Gemini man is often lively and intellectually stimulating. Both value freedom, curiosity, and new experiences, creating a partnership filled with conversations, adventures, and mutual understanding. Their shared love for exploration makes them highly compatible, though they need to ensure they maintain emotional depth alongside their playful nature.

Cancer: A Sagittarius woman and Cancer man may face differences in emotional needs and outlooks on life. She is optimistic and independent, while he tends to be sensitive and nurturing. Building a strong emotional connection requires effort, mutual respect, and understanding of each other's differing perspectives. Their relationship can work if they learn to appreciate their unique qualities.

Leo: This pairing is typically passionate and vibrant. Both signs enjoy socializing, sharing experiences, and expressing themselves confidently. Their shared enthusiasm can lead to a joyful and inspiring relationship. However, both crave attention and admiration, so maintaining a balance of giving and receiving love is essential to prevent jealousy or arrogance.

Virgo: Compatibility between a Sagittarius woman and Virgo man can be complex. She is spontaneous and adventurous, while he is detail-oriented and pragmatic. Their differences can complement each other if they learn from one another; she can bring fun and excitement into his life, and he can offer stability and groundedness. Patience and mutual respect are crucial for harmony.

Libra: A Sagittarius woman and Libra man often form a harmonious and balanced relationship. Both love socializing, intellectual pursuits, and new experiences. Their shared values of fairness and open-mindedness foster understanding and cooperation. They enjoy exploring ideas and adventures together, making their bond both stimulating and stable.

Scorpio: The connection between a Sagittarius woman and Scorpio man can be intense and transformative. While she seeks freedom and exploration, he desires emotional depth and loyalty. Their relationship requires trust and open communication to reconcile these differences. When balanced, they can learn much from each other, experiencing growth and passion.

Sagittarius: Two Sagittarians together often have an energetic, adventurous, and optimistic relationship. Both value independence, exploration, and honesty, which can lead to a partnership filled with excitement and mutual understanding. However, their shared need for freedom must be managed openly to prevent misunderstandings or feelings of neglect.

Capricorn: Compatibility between a Sagittarius woman and Capricorn man can be challenging due to differing priorities. She is free-spirited and desires adventure, while he is ambitious and career-focused. With effort, they can find a way to support each other's goals, blending her enthusiasm with his disciplined approach to life, but it requires mutual compromise.

Aquarius: This pairing often results in a relationship full of innovation, intellectual stimulation, and mutual respect for independence. Both are forward-thinking and value originality, making their connection exciting and unconventional. They inspire each other to grow and explore new ideas, creating a bond based on friendship and shared ideals.

Pisces: A Sagittarius woman and a Pisces man can complement each other emotionally. She brings energy and enthusiasm, helping him step out of his dreams into action, while he offers emotional depth and compassion. Their relationship thrives on mutual understanding and a shared love for exploration, fantasy, and empathy, fostering a nurturing environment.

Capricorn: Ruled by Saturn and an earth sign represents the Sea-Goat..

Chapter 12

Capricorn: (December 22 – January 19)

Male traits: ambitious, disciplined, responsible Influence of Saturn.

What's it like to date a Capricorn man? Dating a Capricorn man can be a fulfilling experience as they are known for their ambition, loyalty, and practicality. Capricorn men are typically ambitious and driven individuals. Show that you appreciate and support his goals and aspirations, and demonstrate that you are willing to stand by his side as he works toward achieving them. Be reliable and responsible. Capricorn men value reliability and responsibility in a partner. Show that you are trustworthy and capable of handling your own responsibilities, as well as being there for him when he needs support. Loyalty is essential for the Capricorn man.

Show him that you are committed to the relationship and that he can trust you to be faithful, honest, and dedicated to building a strong partnership. Capricorn men tend to be grounded in their approach to life, so show your desire for stability and security. Be patient and understanding, as a Capricorn man can be reserved and cautious when it comes to matters of the heart.

How to get a Capricorn man to fall in love with you?

Show your ambition and drive. Capricorn men are attracted to individuals who share their ambition and dedication to success. Loyalty is crucial to a Capricorn man. Show him that you are committed to the relationship and dedicated to building a strong and lasting bond with him. Capricorn men tend to focus on long-term goals, so again, your ability to demonstrate your desire for stability and security is important. By showcasing ambition, reliability, respect for independence, loyalty, and appreciation for practicality, you can capture the heart of a Capricorn man remember to communicate effectively, listen attentively to his needs and concerns, and show genuine interest in building a deep and meaningful connection.

Female traits: Hardworking, traditional, Ambitious Influence of Saturn

What's it like to date a Capricorn woman? Capricorn women appreciate partners who are reliable, responsible, and stable. Demonstrate your commitment to building a solid foundation for the relationship and show that you can be counted on. Respect her ambitions and goals, Capricorn women are driven by nature, so respect her dedication to achieving her success in all aspects of her life. Capricorn women are hardworking and value diligence and perseverance.

Demonstrate your own work ethic and ambition, and show that you are willing to put in the effort to make the relationship thrive. By being reliable, respectful of her ambitions, patient, loyal, and hardworking, you can capture her heart easily.

How to get a Capricorn woman to fall in love with you?

It is essential to understand and appreciate her qualities and preferences. Capricorn women are typically drawn to partners who share their ambition and drive for success. Be patient, they value understanding and patience, especially when it comes to her pace in the relationship. Respect her boundaries and personal space. Allow her freedom to pursue her own interests and goals while being supportive and encouraging. They are smittened by people they can rely on both for emotional support as well as handling challenges together. By being ambitious, patient, loyal, and respect her independence, you can capture her heart. Remember to communicate openly, always attentively listen to her needs, and show a genuine interest in understanding her perspective, this can foster a really deep connection with her.

Capricorn- The Sea Goat

The Sea Goat represents a mythical creature that has the front half of a goat and the tail of a fish. This symbolism combines the characteristics of both animals, emphasizing Capricorn's earth and water elements. The goat represents ambition, determination, practicality, and a strong desire for success and stability. Goats are known for their ability to climb to great heights, which reflects Capricorn's aspiration toward achieving their goals and overcoming obstacles. The fishtail symbolizes the emotional depth and intuition that Capricorns may possess, reminding them of their connection to the inner self and the subconscious mind. Overall, the Sea Goat embodies the qualities of hard work, resilience, and a balanced perspective between the material and emotional aspects of life.

The parts of the body that are associated with the Sea Goat are the bones, knees, and skin. Foods such as yogurts, oranges, bell peppers, green leafy vegetables, and bone broth for collagen are good sources for the Capricorn.

Compatibility Analysis

1. Capricorn Man & Aries Woman

Compatibility: Moderate to High

Strengths: Both are ambitious and driven, making a powerful team. Capricorn's stability balances Aries's energy.

Challenges: Aries's impulsiveness may clash with Capricorn's need for security. Patience and communication are key.

Advice: Focus on shared goals and respect each other's independence.

2. Capricorn Man & Taurus Woman

Compatibility: Very High

Strengths: Both value stability, loyalty, and practicality. They often build a secure, comfortable life together.

Challenges: Possessiveness can sometimes create tension. Both should nurture mutual trust.

Advice: Embrace slow but steady progress in the relationship.

3. Capricorn Man & Gemini Woman

Compatibility: Moderate

Strengths: Gemini's adaptability can inspire Capricorn. They can learn from each other.

Challenges: Differences in communication styles and pace may cause misunderstandings.

Advice: Cultivate patience and find common interests to strengthen bonds.

4. Capricorn Man & Cancer Woman

Compatibility: High

Strengths: Emotional depth of Cancer complements Capricorn's loyalty. They can form a nurturing partnership.

Challenges: Cancer's emotional needs may sometimes overwhelm Capricorn's practicality.

Advice: Open emotional communication enhances their connection.

5. Capricorn Man & Leo Woman

Compatibility: Moderate

Strengths: Leo's enthusiasm can motivate Capricorn. Both are ambitious.

Challenges: Leo's desire for attention vs. Capricorn's reserved nature. Power dynamics may need balancing.

Advice: Celebrate each other's strengths and maintain mutual respect.

6. Capricorn Man & Virgo Woman

Compatibility: Very High

Strengths: Both are practical, detail-oriented, and disciplined. They often understand each other deeply.

Challenges: Perfectionism can cause stress; flexibility is recommended.

Advice: Support each other's goals and maintain open dialogue.

7. Capricorn Man & Libra Woman

Compatibility: Moderate

Strengths: Libra brings charm and diplomacy; Capricorn offers grounding.

Challenges: Different social needs and decision-making styles.

Advice: Find common ground through shared values and interests.

8. Capricorn Man & Scorpio Woman

Compatibility: High

Strengths: Both are intense, committed, and value loyalty.

Challenges: Power struggles or emotional secrecy can surface.

Advice: Transparency and honesty strengthen intimacy.

9. Capricorn Man & Sagittarius Woman

Compatibility: Moderate

Strengths: Sagittarius's optimism can inspire Capricorn's realism.

Challenges: Sagittarius's love for freedom may conflict with Capricorn's need for stability.

Advice: Balance independence with commitment.

10. Capricorn Man & Capricorn Woman

Compatibility: Very High

Strengths: Shared values for tradition, career, stability. They provide mutual support.

Challenges: Both may be overly cautious or work-focused.

Advice: Make time for emotional expression and leisure.

11. Capricorn Man & Aquarius Woman

Compatibility: Moderate

Strengths: Aquarius's innovation complements Capricorn's practicality.

Challenges: Differing social needs; Capricorn's seriousness vs. Aquarius's eccentricity.

Advice: Respect differences; cultivate shared interests.

12. Capricorn Man & Pisces Woman

Compatibility: Moderate

Strengths: Pisces's compassion can soften Capricorn's firmness.

Challenges: Pisces's emotional vulnerability may clash with Capricorn's reserved nature.

Advice: Cultivate emotional openness and patience.

Aries: A Capricorn woman and an Aries man can have an intriguing dynamic. The Capricorn's practicality and disciplined nature can ground the impulsive and energetic Aries. While Aries brings enthusiasm and a zest for adventure, Capricorn offers stability and organization, creating a balance that can work well if both appreciate their differences. Patience and mutual respect are key to building a harmonious relationship.

Taurus: Taurus and Capricorn share an earth element, making them naturally compatible. Both value stability, security, and material comfort, which fosters a strong foundation. Their mutual patience and pragmatic outlooks mean they can build a lasting relationship based on shared goals and values. Loyalty and traditional views often align well, making this pairing very harmonious.

Gemini: Gemini's lively and spontaneous nature can clash with Capricorn's more reserved and disciplined personality. However, with effort, they can complement each other—Gemini can bring lightness to Capricorn's seriousness, while Capricorn can provide grounding for Gemini's flighty tendencies. Communication is essential to bridge their differences.

Cancer: Cancer and Capricorn can form a nurturing and mutually supportive partnership. Cancer's emotional depth complements Capricorn's stability and reliability. Both are caring and protective, and their shared desire for security and family can strengthen their bond. Challenges may arise from Cancer's emotional needs and Capricorn's reserved nature, but understanding and patience are vital.

Leo: Leo's outgoing and attention-loving personality contrasts with Capricorn's more reserved and disciplined demeanor. However, they can learn from each other: Leo can inspire Capricorn to loosen up and enjoy life, while Capricorn can provide Leo with stability and groundedness. Respecting each other's independence and goals is important for this pairing.

Virgo: Virgo and Capricorn share an earth element and a pragmatic outlook, making their compatibility strong. Both are hardworking, detail-oriented, and value organization and stability. Their mutual understanding and shared priorities can lead to a harmonious and productive partnership, often built on trust and shared ambitions.

Libra: Libra's love for harmony, beauty, and social activities may sometimes conflict with Capricorn's focus on work and pragmatism. Nonetheless, they can balance each other if they respect their differences—Libra can introduce a touch of aesthetic and lightness into Capricorn's life, while Capricorn provides structure and discipline to Libra's pursuits. Compromise is essential.

Scorpio: This can be a deep and intense pairing. Both signs value commitment and loyalty. Capricorn's practicality paired with Scorpio's passion can create a powerful bond. Both are driven, ambitious, and value emotional security, making their connection strong if they can navigate differences in emotional expression and trust.

Sagittarius: Sagittarius' love for adventure, freedom, and spontaneity contrasts with Capricorn's cautious and disciplined nature. However, if both remain open-minded, Sagittarius can help Capricorn loosen up, while Capricorn can provide direction and stability. Their relationship thrives on mutual respect for each other's independence.

Capricorn: Two Capricorns together can form a stable, loyal, and ambitious partnership. Both value tradition, responsibility, and long-term goals. While they understand each other's need for structure and success, they should also make space for emotional vulnerability to keep the relationship balanced and fulfilling.

Aquarius: Aquarius' innovative and unconventional approach to life may challenge Capricorn's traditional and cautious outlook. However, their relationship can thrive if they learn from each other—Aquarius can inspire Capricorn to embrace new ideas, while Capricorn can offer groundedness to Aquarius' visions. Mutual respect and shared purpose are important.

Pisces: Pisces' dreamy, empathetic nature complements Capricorn's practicality, offering a balanced blend of realism and emotion. Capricorn provides stability and direction, while Pisces brings imagination and emotional depth. Their differences can be complementary if they communicate openly and nurture patience and understanding.